WHEN DREAMS DIE

JORDYN MERYL

Published by jm dragonfly, L.L.C.
Des Moines, IA
Copyright © April 2012 Jordyn Meryl

This book is a work of fiction. Names, places, characters, and incidents are either the product of the author's imagination, or, if real, used fictitiously. Any resemblance to actual events, locales or persons living or dead is entirely coincidental.

All Rights Reserved. Except for use in any review, the reproduction or utilization of this book in whole or in part in any form, electronic, mechanical or other means, now known or hereafter invented, including photocopying and recording, or in any information storage or retrieval system, is forbidden without the written permission of the author.

ISBN-13:978-1500965969
ISBN-10:1500965960

First Printing: April 2012
Printed in the United States of America
Cover Design-EJR Digital Art-www.ejrdigitalart.com
Author photograph-Trish Toma-Lark

Other Books By Jordyn Meryl

Italian Dream Series
When Dreams Change-Book 1

When Dreams Collide-Book 2

When Dreams Die-Books 3

Becca's Dance
The journey of life is not about the path traveled, but the dance

The Trouble With Angels

Home Before Dark

The Space Between-A Paranormal Romantic Suspense

Coming Soon
Katie's Wind

Silent Running

CHAPTER ONE

"*Damn it, Fernando! You just ruined my sand castle! Go away!*"

The olive-skinned ten year old little girl picked up a hand full of sand and threw it at the boy standing on top of a now pile of sand.

"*I'm going to tell your papa you cussed.*"

This did not help his case. She stood and pushed him back. He landed on his butt in the wet sand. Standing over him, with her hands on her hips, she swung her long black hair back over her shoulder, glared at him with fire coming out of her dark brown eyes. Her slim body shook with anger.

"*Go to hell. I don't care if you tell my father. He would understand.*"

Fernando stood up, brushed the sand from his body. "*Aww, Sophia. I'm sorry. I was just having fun.*"

His puppy-dog eyes always melted her anger. Torn between hitting him or forgiving him, she picked the later. "*Okay...*" *she saw his demure relax.* "*...you are going to help me rebuild it before high tide.*"

His young face broke out into a big grin. "*Great.*"

Sophia kneeled in front of her demolished masterpiece and started to cry. Fernando put his arm around her shoulders. "*It's okay, Sophia. I will help. I can fix things*"

Sophia started giggling. "Fine. But I am the boss. It's my castle."

"Of course."

Together the two worked for hours. Finally they stood back to look at the finish product. Sophia was proud of them. And without admitting it, she knew Fernando had been a big help. Then it came. The big wave crashed over the sand castle, and when it receded all that was left was a smooth surface. Fernando took hold of Sophia's hand. She squeezed it.

"Thank you." She whispered as she laid her head on his shoulder.

"You're welcome." His soft boyish voice always made her feel good, safe, protected.

***

Sophia sat on the rugged rocks, throwing small pebbles into the crashing waves. Looking to her left, she saw the familiar figure walking the shoreline.

Fernando

Sophia couldn't remember a time she didn't love him. The quieter one of the cousins, he was always there for her. The other two liked to play games, always tease each other with jokes, rough housing. But Fernando would spend hours in Sophia's garden reading books, playing board games.

Not that he wasn't as gorgeous has the other two. His silky black hair, caramel skin and mink colored eyes could weaken the knees of any girl or woman. He was slim and tall. He surfed, swam and boated. Not as a competition, as a skill he loved to pursue.

As he closed the distance between them, a smile lit up his handsome face. It also gave Sophia the grounding she needed. He was her rock, solid strong. With him she would always feel safe. From their childhood, his 'I can fix things' words always rang true. He fixed her. When she fell and got hurt, he took the pain away. If she was sick, he sat by her bed until she felt better.

***

When Sophia was twelve, her mother just left one day. No reason, no good bye, no explanation. She just woke up one day and her father told her at breakfast that her mother would never be back.

His tone spoke of the finalization of the announcement. Sophia knew better than to ask him why. Her father was a sturdy, uncompromising man who never allowed questions. Finishing her meal in silence, she watched his face. He frowned as he looked out the windows in the eating nook that they were sharing. Sophia wanted to reach out and touch his hand, comfort him, but she decided against it.

Excusing herself, she ran down to the beach. Fernando was riding the early morning waves. Still in her night gown, she jumped up and down on the beach, waving at him. He saw her, nodded his head and rode the next wave in.

Sophia sunk down to the wet sand. Fernando walked from the water, like a god, carrying his board under his arm. Throwing it down, he went to his knees, grabbing her by her arms.

His face full of fear. "What's wrong, Sophia?"

"My...mother...is gone." Her words came out stiff between the sobs.

"Gone? Gone where?" His grip tighten.

Sophia shook her head, her eyes locked with his. "I don't know."

A frown creased his face. "Who told you this?"

"Papa."

"And what did he say?"

"Just 'your mother is gone'."

Fernando was silent. Drawing her into his chest, he stoked her back with the salt water dripping from his body. Sophia snuggled deep into him. His body warmed the ice in her soul.

Then his words warmed her heart. "It's okay, Sophia. I will fix this."

While he never fixed her mother leaving, he did fix Sophia. Letting her vent at him, instead of her dad carried her through the painful experience.

***

Now seven years later, Fernando still fixed things. And in two months she would be his wife. They created a plan and he kept the plan on track. That's what Fernando did for her. However once in awhile, she would shake things up. While her father picked a different college for her, she and Fernando always found a way to sneak away and meet.

Since her mother left, Vito kept her on a short leash, and she allowed it. There was a deep, unspoken fear of not crossing him. She believed he loved her, but he didn't show in any affectionate way. So he spoiled her. She never wanted for anything, except her freedom.

And marrying Fernando would give her that. They were going to live in the same village as Alejandro and Jessica. Fernando had a teaching job, Sophia had been hired by a small architectural firm that created fantastic designs. Her father had bought them a house when he finally figured out that she was going to do this, with or without his blessing.

Jumping off the rock, she ran the remaining distance and flew into his arms. Pressing her body into his,

When Dreams Die

he wrapped one arm around her and drew her in. His kiss was magical as always.

In his arms, Sophia found her world. She returned his kiss with a tease of things to come. "Let's go to the cave."

He smiled his boyish grin that had taken many a woman down. "You're on."

Running hand in hand, they jutted between the rocks, ducking down to enter the mouth of a very isolated cave they had found it years ago as children. At first it was their secret place where no one could find them. Then it became their love cave, where they could enjoy each other in privacy and peace.

Sophia had hid a quilt in one of the many holes in the walls. As she removed it, Fernando took candles from another hole, placing them around in the sand. A CD player rested on a ledge, she pressed the button to start the music.

Turning to Fernando, she watched as he removed his shirt. His rock hard chest glistened in the candlelight. Strolling up to him, her hands roamed over his skin. Laying soft butterfly kisses on him, he groaned as he took her with him to the quilt. Untying the front of her dress, her breast broke free. There was no underwear to interfere with his undressing her.

Her body loved his touch. It responded on its own, sending hot flames down to lick her core. His hands traveled down to connect with her fire. Lying naked under him, the warm sea air caressed her skin. The soft sounds of the waves, mixed with the music took her to a place of peace. For this man was her world and she could never get enough of him.

She arched and squirmed under his body. He teased her with his tongue, forcing her desire to climb. Protected in their own secret spot, he took his time. Moving her hands over his body, she touched his manhood and felt the hardness. He wanted her as much as she wanted him.

He paused. "Tell me what you want."

Sophia sighed. This was his way of bringing her to an exploding climax. The tension climbed in her. "I want you."

"To do what?"

"To make love to me."

He licked the inside of her thigh. "Here?"

The movement took her breath away. "Yes."

He licked the other side. "Here?"

Her womanhood jerked. The sweet feeling of anticipation crested over her. She wanted him to both hurry and take his time. Then he licked her hot spot. She screamed as the orgasm grabbed her, sending her up over the cliff. He probed deeper as one then another crashed up her body.

She begged him. He pressed again, setting in motion another wave of pleasure. Digging her nails into his back, she hung on for dear life.

Then he entered her. Slow, then faster as the last climax, stronger than the others broke through her. "Oh, god."

His came at the same time, as he always did. Fernando knew the right timing. The right spots. The right way.

And Sophia knew he would always please her. As they lay together, she licked the sweat off his arm.

When he rolled off, he gathered her to him. The coolness of the damp sand filtered up though the blanket cooling their naked bodies. The sounds of sea and the warmth of the breeze surrounded them, giving them the feeling that they were the only people in the world. Falling into a light sleep, Sophia enjoyed the quiet moment with her lover.

***

Fernando walked Sophia to her villa, arm in arm. She slipped her hand down and took his. At the garden, he unlatched the old, iron gate, it screeched as it reluctantly swung open. Sophia's garden was a place of great natural beauty and peace. She had hired an old man from the village who had a reputation for being able to grow anything. Everyday Signor Da Vinci would come and tend the plants. Some say he was a descendent of Leonardo, that he processed the magic of the artist in his ability to grow things. True or not, Sophia gave him the run of the garden. In her mind, it was a tribute to her mother, Raffaella.

Sophia had never accepted her father's story about her mother's disappearance. As a child, she had memories of the beautiful woman who spilled her love onto the small child. Never did Sophia ask her father again where her mother went. But in her heart she knew something was not right about what she had been told.

The couple walked hand in hand through the arches and cobblestone paths to Sophia's bedroom door. Fernando put his hand behind Sophia's neck, lowered his head to kiss her. She molded into his body. Parting was hard and she longed for the day she didn't have to leave him at night.

His parting words were spoken against her lips. "Good night love, sleep well."

Sophia smiled. Little did he know, she would sleep well when he slept beside her. "Same to you."

She stood as he ran his hand down her arm, then stepped back. His eyes spoke of his love for her. It was something she could always believe in. He walked away, she stood there until he vanished through the gate. Looking up at the moon, she leaned against the door jam.

Mama, wherever you are, thank you for giving me Fernando.

She turned and went into her room. Slithering out of her clothes, she slipped her gown over her head. Starting for her bed, she smiled.

I'm hungry. Making love with Fernando creates an appetite.

Pulling a robe from the hook, she went out the door, down the hall. As she reached the top of the stairs, she heard heavy male voices coming from her dad's study. Grabbing the railing, she walked softly, her bare feet making no sound as she descended. The voices could be heard behind the half closed door. Reaching the bottom, she narrowed her eyes to see through the gap in the door. Her father's back was to her, in front of him was a man she had seen before, but didn't know. The man saw her, spoke to her father. Vito turned and was not pleased to see his daughter standing there. He jerked around, walking to the door.

"What are you doing up, Sophia?"

Sophia pointed her thumb over her shoulder. "I was just getting something to eat. Is everything alright, Papa?"

With his hand on the door, Vito nodded. "Everything is fine. Good night Sophia." With his final words he shut the door in her face. She heard the lock click.

An uneasy feeling came over her. Like something wasn't right. She couldn't put her finger on what it was, but... The reasons flew from her mind.

***

During the warm months, Sophia ate her breakfast alone on the terrace. She stopped joining her father when she came home from college. Facing him over a table had become uncomfortable, so she weaned herself away. Besides, they had little to say to each other. Every year Sophia saw her father withdraw from her a little more. Plus, they had nothing to talk about. He didn't want to share his world with her and she preferred he not be part of hers. The underlining distrust grew every day. Now it was a wall that blocked them from each other.

Concetta, their cook, prepared Sophia her breakfast every morning, except Sunday. Sundays Concetta went to early Mass. Sophia would meet Fernando in the village at a local coffee shop. Then they went to a later Mass together. Sophia always lit a candle and prayed for her mother, it was a ritual that gave her some kind of comfort.

This morning, Sophia walked out into a beautiful, cool, sunny, early fall morning. The view from her spot was break taking. The sea stretched out to meet the sky. The colors of dawn still lingered, but the day promised to be clear. Concetta had the food ready for Sophia. Sitting down, a young girl around seven came to the table and poured the first cup of coffee. The brown liquid swirled to a light tan as cream was added.

Sophia smiled at the child. "And who would you be?"

The dark haired girl blushed under her olive skin. "I am Neve. Concetta is my grandmamma." Her voice was low, sweet and young.

"Helping out?"

"Si. I like to spend time with grandmamma and I love your villa."

Sophia chuckled at the honesty. "Well, enjoy yourself." Taking her first sip, she winked at the girl. "Thanks for the coffee."

Neve sat the coffee pot on the table, curtsied. Smiling at Sophia, she hurried back into the house.

Sophia's cell phone rang. For all the old charm of the countryside, Sophia had connected to the new century with all the technology available.

"Hello?"

"Sophia, Jane here from the Naples. My assistant is ready to finalize the wedding plans. You available?"

"Yes, I can come to the city today. Give me a couple of hours. I will meet her at the shop."

"Great." Jane clicked off.

Sophia opened the notebook that had become a constant companion in the last few months. She didn't really want the big wedding, she just wanted to marry Fernando as soon as possible. But, her position in the village and her father's rank in the community dictated she put on a major event. So far, the wedding included three days of festivities. People from all over the world were coming. She finished her breakfast in a hurry and walked into the kitchen.

"Concetta." Sophia's words made the woman stop her chopping and turn around. Wiping her hands on her apron, she awaited her instructions. "I am going to the city. I won't be back for lunch."

"Dinner?"

Sophia paused for a minute. "Probably not. I hope to catch up with Fernando, might meet him at Jessica's." Sophia shook her head. "Don't count on me."

Walking pass Neve, Sophia leaned down and looked the little girl in the eyes. "Have a good day. Try to get some time in the pool, it's wonderful."

Straightening up, Sophia winked at Concetta. "Enjoy your day."

Concetta sighed. "I'll try. Signor Rossi is having guest for dinner."

Sophia frowned. "Really? Then I know I will be gone."

Bouncing out of the room, she sprinted up the stairs to her room. Grabbing her purse, she also gathered a messenger bag, stuffing her notebook in it as she went back down the stairs. Half running out to the large garage that housed many cars, Sophia jumped in the Maserati. Pulling it outside, she lowered the top of the convertible. Feeling the sun on her face, she grabbed her long hair and put it in a hair tie. Finishing the ritual with designer sun glasses, she gunned the motor and flew down the driveway, waving at the gardener as she sped by.

The coastal highway welcomed the openness of the road. Sophia could feel her heart racing. Working on the wedding plans brought her closer to the day she would be able to live with Fernando. The promise of such freedom livened her spirits.

Just bide your time, girl. A wonderful, simple life awaits you.

She pushed on the gas pedal, tuned up the radio with some Italian rock and sang out.

***

The dress Sophia picked was a simple halter top in white satin. No frills, no lace, no train. Ribbons criss-crossed over her bare back. Trying it on for the third and last time, it fit her slim body perfectly. Her veil was a lace head cover she found in a trunk in the attic. She remembered her mother wearing it to Mass. She had taken it to a seamstress in the village to clean.

***

The old woman held the veil in her hands, stroking it tenderly. "This is very old."

"It was my mother's" Sophia spoke with pride.

The old lady's face softened as she kept her eyes on the veil. "I remember her wearing it. I believe it was her grandmother's"

Sophia was surprised at the old woman's words. "You knew my mother?"

"Si. Her family settled here centuries ago." The old woman nodded as she still stroked the fragile lace.

"Are there any left?" Sophia felt hope jump up. Maybe she could find her mother.

"No, they have all died or left since..." The old lady jerked her head up quickly, looking around the shop. "They are all gone."

Sophia felt something was not being said. She waited, hoping the old lady would tell her more.

But she didn't. "It will be a pleasure to get this ready for your wedding."

Sophia was disappointed that the subject was closed. "Thank you."

***

Placing the veil over her head, the lace fell in folds touching her cheek, her bare shoulders, down her back to the floor. It felt like it was encompassing her with love. Her eyes misted.

Oh Mama. I can't believe you wouldn't be here for my wedding day if you could.

The wedding assistant stood back, her arms folded. "You look beautiful."

Sophia smiled. "Thank you, and for all you've done. It's just one more week, then the madness will be over."

Stepping down from the rise she stood on, Sophia picked up the skirt and walked to the dressing room. "I am pleased with the dress, I will take it with me."

Redressing, Sophia walked out into the show room. "Now, what else needs attention?"

The assistant and Sophia sat at a table and went through the check list. Everything was crossed off including the tuxes and the bridesmaid's dresses, for two of Sophia's friends from college. The ceremony would be in the local church, the reception at the villa. Over a thousand people would attend the event. The village would be closed except for the locals that would be helping.

One week. And she would be Signora Giordano.

***

Sitting at the kitchen counter at Bella's, Sophia nibbled on garlic crackers. Bella moved around the kitchen, preparing the evening meal. "How are the wedding plans going?"

Sophia smiled. "Done, I finalized everything first of the week."

"Your dress?" Bella talked as she worked, always on the move.

Sophia watched as Bella fussed. "Hanging in my room, ready."

"And your father?" A small bite in her words.

Sophia frowned. Bella and Vito had grown up in the same village, but not in the same way. While they were polite, Sophia always got the feeling they did not like each other. "He's fine I guess. I know his custom ordered tux arrived and he paid all the bills so he's doing his job."

Bella turned and chuckled. "So everything is set. Tonight the rehearsal dinner, tomorrow the wedding and then...?"

Sophia took a deep breath. "Then the madness will be over and Fernando and I will begin our own life together."

Bella came over and patted Sophia's cheek. "Honeymoon?"

"We are going to the mountains. Since we live on the beach we decided to go up."

Bella smiled. "And you will live down by Alejandro and Jessica?"

Sophia nodded. "Yes, we both have jobs there and family. Well, your family."

"What about your brother?" Bella turned back to the oven, removing a tray of pastries.

Sophia felt a pang of sadness. "Paolo will come to the wedding, but then he will go back to France. He promised he would tolerate our father for me. That's all I can ask."

Bella sat the tray on the counter. "Is he coming tonight?"

Gladness erupted inside Sophia. "Yes, he should be arriving soon. Thank you for letting him stay here."

Bella shook her head. "Not a problem, I miss him also.

The two women turned at the sound of the front door opening and a familiar voice yelling. "Anyone here to welcome home the lost son?"

Sophia jumped off the stool, running towards the voice. Rounding the corner, she saw her older brother standing there. As soon as he saw her he dropped his bags, opened his arms as she leaped into them. Swinging her around, her arms locked around his neck.

Burying her face in his neck, the familiar smell of musk soap reminded her of the days before he left. "Paolo. I have missed you so."

He stopped moving and set her down. "You too, sis. Let me look at you."

***

Paolo left home right after her mother did. For years, Sophia didn't hear from him, so she fantasized they were together. But, that dream ended when she looked him up as soon as she left for college.

Sophia sat at the small French café drinking her glass of wine. She had been nervous when she called Paolo to meet with her. He had suggested the meeting place, giving her directions. The wine was sweet and calming. She was so sure he would come with her mother, she could hardly sleep the night before. This was her ultimate dream, that the two of them would come and she would again have her family back.

She didn't care what her father thought. If he couldn't accept Paolo and Raffaella, then he needed to exit her life. Holding her tongue and pretending that the obvious did not exist was over. As soon as she felt her mother's arms around her, she would stand up to her father.

A dashing figure of a man stood across the street. Sophia smiled to herself. It was her charming brother, as adorable as she imagined. Straining her neck, she did not see anyone with him, the hope in her chest collapsed. Their mother was not with him, meaning all the expectations she had built up in her mind just crashed and burned.

Watching him dart across the busy street, she fought back tears of frustration. Standing so he could see her, a broad smile took his face over. Jogging to her, he took her in his arms and gave her a long bear hug.

His voice was deeper than she imagined, but then he had become a man in place of the boy she had last seen. "Sophia, you are beautiful. You have grown into a lovely woman."

She couldn't hide her disappointment. "I was hoping Mama was with you." Her voice caught in her throat.

Paolo eyes softened as he stroked her cheek, wiping a tear away with his thumb. "No, baby, she's gone forever." Her eyes begged him to tell her the truth, but that is all he ever said. The subject never came up again.

They kept in touch for the four years she was in school. Fernando went with her sometimes when she traveled to France to see

Paolo. Sophia never told her father she saw her brother. He never asked and she figured he didn't care so why tell him.

***

But today was a happy day. Years of waiting would end tomorrow. Tonight they celebrated.

Bella had followed Sophia. Sophia stepped back as Bella hugged Paolo patting his face. "You are still very handsome. But your face..." she grabbed his chin, shook it. "...it is as if the gods have chiseled it themselves."

Paolo laughed. "It is always good to see you Mama Bella."

As they hugged, Fernando slipped up behind Sophia, wrapped his arms around her waist, pulling her close, whispering in her ears. "Now this will make the next few days exciting."

She jokingly nudged him with her elbow. She knew he knew how much it meant to her to have Paolo there. He also knew the bad blood between her father and brother. But she knew, with all confidence, that he supported her and would do whatever made her happy.

CHAPTER TWO

Sophia adjusted the flowing black dress that hugged her slim figure, moving it back and forth. Looking at herself in the full length mirror, she grinned.

Now it is down to hours before Fernando is my husband.

She glanced around her bedroom. Most of her important belongings had been packed and delivered to their new house, the room looked strangely bare. All that remained of hers was the wedding dress and the things she would need for the wedding tomorrow. Tonight would be her last night in this room that had been her life from birth. But there were no regrets for leaving, just for staying so long.

A soft knock on the door. "Sophia?"

"Come in Papa." Sophia gathered the sheer, hand painted Pashmina shawl around her shoulders.

As he entered, she turned to face him. "I am ready."

Vito took in a sigh. "You look like..." Sophia saw a sliver of pain cross his eyes. "...very beautiful."

Sophia slipped her arm through his. "Thank you Papa." Guiding him to the door, she released him and walked ahead. Down the grand staircase, she saw the two men who were always with her father. They never talked to her, seldom made eye contact. She thought sometimes they were different men, they all looked the same, dark suits, dark glasses, never a smile. The only words she ever heard from them were addressed to Vito.

At the foot of the stairs, she again slipped her arm in her father's. Always, she had felt uneasy about the so called "associates". Gliding by them, she and Vito walked outside. The evening light was just starting, the sky a beautiful array of colors.

While Sophia's morning view was of the sun rising over the sea, the evening sun set on the luscious green hills of the vineyard, both took her breath away. Still, the village she and Fernando would live in had a sea and lovely mountains at her back.

One of the men in black opened the back door of her father's car, a black Mercedes. Sophia sat down on the luscious leather. Vito sat next to her. During the ride, no body spoke. The quiet was welcome to Sophia, it seemed she never had anything to say to her father. Less words spoken, the less lies. For, since her mother left, Sophia had never believed her father's words again. His eyes spoke of his betrayal. She saw it every day and was grateful she wouldn't have to hide her angry, unspoken words anymore.

Pulling into Bella's driveway, the circle was full of cars. Sophia first saw Fernando waiting for her on the steps. His handsome face broke into a smile as he spotted her car. As the car pulled up in front of him, he opened her door before Vito's man even got out. Taking her hand, he gave her the look that told her she was safe now.

Sophia swung her legs out and stood. Fernando kissed her cheek. "Ready for all of this?"

As they climbed the steps ahead of her father and one of his men, the other stayed with the car, she leaned into Fernando. "Where's Paolo?"

"In the back with Roberto and Alejandro. Did you tell your father he is here?"

"No." She glanced back. "I figured he could find out in a crowd, that way he wouldn't make a scene. I least I think not."

Fernando nodded. "Nice."

The patio was lined with small, twinkling lights, one long table set with the family china. A bar sat at one end, Sophia saw Jessica, Alejandro, Roberto and Emily standing together. Turning to her left she saw Paolo talking to her bridesmaids. He turned to look at her, a smile on his face that faded as his eyes looked beyond her.

"What the hell?" Sophia heard her father's angry voice.

Stiffening, she tightened her grip on Fernando's arm. He moved his body closer in a protective mode. Paolo frowned then looked back at his sister and nodded.

Vito's voice ripped behind her. "I need a drink." He and his man walked towards the bar. Fernando's cousins welcomed him, but Sophia could see the humor in their eyes, knowing they understood the situation and were willing to work with it.

Sophia nudged Fernando toward her brother. Going to the group, she hugged Paolo. "Thanks."

"Only for you sis. You know that?"

"I do." Sophia turned and hugged her bridesmaids.

Bella's voice sounded over the crowd. "Dinner. Find your place cards, sit there. No switching."

According to custom, Sophia and Fernando sat at the head, Vito sat on Sophia's right, Fernando's parents on his left. On down it went. Paolo sat with Alejandro and everyone else at the far end of the table.

Sophia sighed.

Good for now. This would be the only time her father and brother had to be together. Except maybe her funeral, then she didn't care.

A chill went down her back, but she shook it off.

***

Unable to sleep all night, Sophia rose before dawn. Going down to the kitchen she found Concetta already cooking. Putting her hands on the sweet woman's shoulder she kissed her cheek.

"Good morning. Why are you here so early?"

"This is the biggest day of your life, little one. I must prepare a good breakfast for you."

Sophia poured fresh, hot coffee into a cup, finishing off with a large dose of heavy cream, she smiled as she took her first sip. Concetta was probably the closest thing she had to a caretaker in this house. Sophia's material and physical needs were always met.

Bella and Gina had tried to guide the young girl through the web of becoming a woman, she guessed she could say she had different women providing different aspects of her upbringing. As grateful as she was to them, she would have liked to have just one mother.

Still, they all had a part in helping her reach this day and for that she was grateful. Looking out the large window to her favorite view, she knew this would be the last time it welcomed her in the morning.

"Coffee is good." Sophia heard the crack in her voice.

Concetta was pounding dough on a wooden board. "Grazie." Always a woman of few words, Concetta kept the rhythm of her pounding.

Today, Sophia felt words needed to be said. She walked over, lightly put her hand on the older woman's arm stopping the motion. Concetta looked up with questions in her eyes.

"You are very dear to me." Sophia saw the wetness come to Concetta's eyes. "I will never be able to thank you for being there for me."

Concetta didn't answer, she just nodded. Footsteps sounded behind them. Sophia removed her hand, Concetta returned to her work. Vito entered the kitchen, still in his robe, his hair wet from his routine morning shower.

"What time does all this start today?" His voice gruff and harsh.

Sophia chuckled. "Good morning to you too, father. We leave the house at nine o'clock. The ceremony starts at ten."

"It doesn't take an hour to get to the village." He shuffled over to the coffee pot.

Sophia sat down at the counter. "No, but we need to arrive early so I can get dressed."

He looked over the rim of his cup at her. "Dressed? Why can't you dress here?"

Sighing, she fought hard to keep it civil. "Because, I am getting dressed at the church. You however, need to be in your tux. You will be greeting the guests."

"Why? They know me." Vito hunched his shoulders.

Keeping it polite, Sophia kept her eyes on her father's face. "I'm sure they do, but it's customary."

"Fine." He took a cup of coffee to the breakfast nook.

Sophia looked over at Concetta, they both were holding back their laughter. Concetta slid the tray of pastries into the oven. Sophia left to go back upstairs with her coffee.

***

With the wedding dress draped over her arms, Sophia took one last look at her room. Guilt almost made her sorry for wanting to leave. She smiled and shook off the feeling. Going out to the hallway, she carefully took one step at a time down the grand staircase. Finally, feeling both feet on the floor, she hiked up her load. One of her father's men held the front door open for her, the other met her on the steps and took the dress from her aching arms.

Sophia nodded, thankful for the help. "Hang it in the back for me, please."

The man bowed. He held it with care, carrying it as if it were the precious cargo that it was. Sometimes Sophia wished they wore name tags so she could at least put a name to the face. Her father never introduced them, never called them by any name. The man hung the dress on the hook, stood back for Sophia to enter.

"Thank you..." She left the sentence unfinished.

Sophia had put on jeans and a t-shirt for the ride to the church. Settling into the seat of the limo, she took a breath and leaned back. Turning her head towards the still opened door, she saw her father come down the steps, looking very dapper in his tux. She smiled and patted his arm as he sat next to her. "You look very nice, Papa."

His eyes looked straight ahead as he nodded to the driver. The car pulled away from the house, traveling down the long driveway. Sophia looked out the window as the places of her childhood passed by. Through the large iron gate, the car turned left, going down the hill, passing the rows of grapes. The village popped up in the distance. Sophia and her father did not talk, which did not surprise her. They never had many words for each other.

True to form, the ride only lasted fifteen minutes. Arriving at the church, the driver pulled up at the front doors. The other man opened the car door for Vito. Not waiting for someone to open her door, Emily bounced out of the car. Walking around the other side of the car, she supervised the man taking the dress out. He held it in both his arms like a delicate child.

She motioned him to follow her, going up the wide church steps, to open the heavy wooden double doors. As she held the door for him, he entered the dark, serene foyer. Working her way around him, she heard his footsteps follow her. Going to the side room reserved as her dressing room, she held the door for him.

She pointed to a large hook on the wall. "Over there."

He lifted the dress by the hanger and placed it on the hook.

"Thank you..." Still, no name.

He nodded, walked sternly out the door. Sophia closed the door behind him, leaning against it.

So far so good.

A light tap on the door startled her. "Sophia, it's Beth." Beth was here to do her hair and make-up.

Opening the door, she smiled. "Come in." Prep time was here.

***

An hour later, the room was filled with women. Her two bridesmaids were putting on their finishing touches. Sophia had chosen a blue to match the color of the sea for the dresses. Soft and flowing, they matched well with the gray tuxes. The feeling of an ancient Roman era gave Sophia thoughts of her roots. She was grounded in this country of wine and sea. She never had a desire to leave Italy.

"Show time girls!" The wedding planner clapped her hands. Sophia placed the lace veil on her head, the final touch to her dress. As the women left, Sophia stood looking in the mirror at her reflection. What she saw was not her image, but the years of waiting for this day. Her stomach fluttered as the realization hit her. Vito appeared behind her.

His face was drawn. "You look like your mother the day I married her." He touched the lace on her veil. A frown creased his forehead.

Sophia watched his reaction. "It was hers."

His head jerked up. "How did you find it?" His tone held an edge.

Biting her lip, she kept her eyes on him. "In the attic."

His face took on a sad look. "She wore it on her wedding day."

So many questions jumped across Sophia's mind, but this wasn't the time or place. Nor did it matter anymore. The past was just that. Gone. No words, explanations or justification could change that.

Sophia shook the bad thoughts from her head. Turning, she took her father's arm. "Let's go, Papa."

He nodded. She noticed the pain in his eyes, but she had no sympathy for him. Whatever had happened she was sure it was his fault.

Together, they walked out into the foyer. The wedding procession stood at attention, a waiting the go-ahead. Sophia nodded to the wedding planner. Without words, she started the line down the aisle: Flower girl, ring bearer, bridesmaids. As Sophia and her father entered the doorway, she looked down the aisle to Fernando.

Handsome in his gray tux, he smiled at her and the world was right again. As they stepped on the white runner, crushing rose petals under their feet, Sophia and her father took their one and only walk together. Sophia didn't even notice the guests, her heart was way ahead of her, with Fernando down at the altar. She couldn't get there quick enough.

As Vito handed her over, she gripped her groom's hand for strength. Fernando drew her to his side, giving her the smile that always ripped chills to her toes. The warmth of his hand, the feel of his body next to her, allowed her to release the breath she had unconsciously

When Dreams Die

been holding. Listening to the priest's words, she could only smile. Trusting and loving Fernando was the easy part.

"I do." The words flowed from her mouth.

As he placed the ring on her finger, she felt the warmth of his love in his touch.

"You may kiss the bride."

As their lips touched, Sophia wanted to shout, but instead whispered against his lips. "I so love you, Fernando Giordano."

"And Sophia Giordano, I will love you all the days of my life and beyond."

The guests were on their feet, clapping. The couple turned and faced the crowd. Sophia felt a smile explode on her face. Walking back down the aisle she saw Jessica and Emily, standing next to Paolo.

She reached out her hand and touched Paolo's, mouthing the words. "I love you." He nodded back.

Stepping out into the sunlight, Sophia saw the horse drawn carriage, decorated with white roses and gardenias. The people came out of the church, throwing flower petals at the couple. They flowed on down the steps, surrounding the carriage, into the street.

Fernando led her to the carriage. Lifting her up, he followed her to the seat. Waving to all their friends and family, the driver clicked the reins and the horse started down the street to Bella's villa. Out of sight of the church, Sophia raised her arms over her head, lifted her face to the sun and shouted. "I am married, at last!"

Fernando drew her into his arms and kissed her with longing and passion kiss. A car horn startled the newlyweds. Sophia turned to look back over her shoulder. A long line of cars followed the slow moving carriage. Laughing, the couple waved at their entourage.

***

Bella's villa glistened in the afternoon light. The carriage stopped at the foot of the steps to the front door. The cars moved around, parking all over the large circle driveway. Several vans from the village stood in a line next to the lawn, carrying signs that advertised food, flowers and rental services.

Fernando helped Sophia climb down. Once on the ground, they walked up the steps. The wedding planner greeted them, positioning them for the receiving line, the bride and groom stood at the end followed by the groomsmen and bridesmaids, then the parents.

Sophia saw Paolo silently slide into the house. He gave her a smile and she nodded back. Her brother had honored her wishes to not fight with their father. She knew Paola carried a deep seated hatred for Vito. Their mother leaving must have hurt him as much as her, he just never talked about it. Well, that was high on her list, to talk honestly and openly with her brother about their mother's departure.

After a while, Sophia leaned out and looked at the line. Seeing the end, she stretched and took a deep breath.

Fernando turned at the sound of her sigh. "Do you see the end?"

Nodding, she raised her eyebrows. "I do."

He loosened his tie. "Good, I could use something to drink."

Sophia smiled. "I would like to just sit down and have something cool to drink...Ah here is the last person."

Sophia hugged a long-lost second cousin once removed, she had no idea what her name was. As she watched the stranger walk away, she took Fernando's hand. She hadn't even caught her breath when the wedding planner ushered them through the house to the wedding party table.

A long table was set for all the members. Jessica and Emily joined their men at the table. Her bridesmaids sat with their dates. Fernando's parents sat at the table, as did Vito on Sophia's right. He sat alone, without his men or a date. In fact Sophia never saw him date. No woman ever crossed her path at the villa or out in public, for that she was grateful.

The lawn stretched out in front of the table, dotted with white tents, the bright blue sea as the back drop. The day was perfect, a clear sky, a cool breeze and happy people. Searching over the crowd, Sophia spotted Paolo sitting at a table with some of their childhood friends. She caught his eye, smiled, he nodded. The unspoken language of brother and sister.

The festivities began. Food and wine flowed at every table.

Alejandro, as the best man, stood and offered a toast. "To Fernando and the love of his life, Sophia. May you have many happy moments, and many children. Salute!" Laughter rang out as everyone lifted their glasses.

Fernando squeezed Sophia's hand, whispered in her ear. "Yes, many children."

A warmth spread through her.

Yes, many children. And a mother that will never leave them for any reason.

Sophia kissed Fernando's cheek. "I love you."

The dimple in his cheek deepened as he smiled. "The same." A standing joke with them, she laughed at the humor.

***

After a feast fit for a king, the evening shades beckoned the couple to perform their first dance together. Walking to the dance floor, Sophia flowed into Fernando's arms. Looking only at him, she rubbed the back of his neck. Remaining unaware of anyone around them, she had eyes only for her new husband.

Cocking her head, she smiled. "Did you think this day would ever come?"

Fernando's eyes sparkled. "Always. I can't remember ever not knowing I would marry you."

Sophia licked her bottom lip. "This is the beginning of our life together. Just you and me."

Throwing back his head, he laughed. "And the whole Giordano family."

"I love all your family. I have considered them my family since..."

Sophia remembered coming to Bella's, talking to her and Gina about the woman things she did not have a mother to ask.

She shook the thought from her head. "...forever."

Fernando drew her close. "You have always been part of this family. It will be a minor change."

"Except..." the excitement tingled her stomach. "...we will live by ourselves, creating our own branch of the family..." she winked at him. "...so to speak."

A tap on her shoulder interrupted their dance. Stepping away from Fernando, Sophia turned to see her father standing there. "Papa?"

Vito rubbed his forehead. "Gina said I was next to dance with you."

Gina appeared next to him. "Yes, and I get to dance with my handsome son." She nodded towards Vito. Sophia accepted the instruction. For the sake of tradition, she would follow the protocol.

Walking into her father's arms, Sophia felt stiff. It had been years, maybe never she had been in his arms. Never any hugs, kisses, nothing especially since...

She remembered her manners. "Papa, you look very handsome today."

Vito grunted. "I see you invited your brother."

Sophia braced for the repercussion. "Yes. We wanted him here." She softened her tone. "Be good, please. You two are the only family I have."

Her father was not accustomed to obeying any orders or requests not his own. Sophia stared him down as she waited for his response.

His eyes reflected acceptance. "Fine. For you princess."

Sophia frowned, he hadn't used that term of endearment since she was a small child.

Let it go.

"Thank you, Papa." She buried her head on his shoulder. If there was one thing she learned from her father it was to always be gracious, even if you wanted to let your anger out.

The awkward dance ended quickly. Several more of the wedding party and family came to dance with her, but she kept her eyes on Paolo. He was pretending to ignore his obligation to dance with her. Finally, she maneuvered her last partner over to her brother's spot. When the music changed and so did the partners, she held out her arms to Paolo.

He shook his head.

She nodded. "Yes. It's time."

Giving her a sideways look, he stood, took her in his arms. "I saw you dancing with the old man. What did he say?"

Sophia glanced towards her father. "He called me princess."

Paola pulled back, searched her face, frowned. "He did?"

"Yes. And it was too little too late. I am now Fernando's wife. And I will create a family far removed from him."

Paola eyes twinkled. "And where am I in this family of yours?"

Sophia laughed. "You are the amazing Uncle Paolo. I expect to be pampered when I am pregnant. And all my children showered with lavish gifts."

He pulled back to look at her. "And how many children are we talking about here?"

"Many." Sophia smiled at her older brother. "And I want to see more of you. In fact..." Fernando stepped in and stopped their dance. "What are the two of you talking about?"

When Dreams Die

Sophia slipped into her new husband's arms. "About how we want to see more of my illusive brother."

Fernando nodded. "Indeed."

Paola smiled at the couple.

"In fact..." Sophia looked at Fernando, then Paolo. "...I am formally inviting you to Sunday brunch in two weeks. At our villa."

Paolo started to protest, but Sophia put her index finger on his lips. "No excuses. Just be there. Bring wine."

Paola chuckled. "Okay, I will be there. With wine."

***

Changing out of her wedding dress, Sophia hung it with care on the hanger. Bella wanted to preserve it for her, so it was staying here, but the lace veil was staying with her. She felt close to her mother when she wore it. As it caressed her hair and touched her face, she could imagine the feel her mother's hands.

Pulling up her jeans, she snapped them, grabbed a sweater from the bed. Fernando was waiting on the balcony just outside. Picking up her bouquet, she took one last sniff of the flowers. Walking out to join Fernando, he turned as he heard the doors open.

Going to the banister, below them was an overview of the reception area and beyond. A sea of young women gathered to catch the bouquet. Smiling down at the crowd, Sophia noticed two dark figures on the outskirts. They appeared to be in a heated argument.

That's my father and Paolo.

"Fernando..." Sophia grabbed his arm, pulled him to her. "That's Papa and Paolo."

Pitching her flowers out to the people waiting, she bolted. Down the stairs and out the doors, she was on a dead run for the two men. As they came into sight, she saw Alejandro and Roberto stepping between.

Angry words floated back to her. "You can't deal with the truth old man!" Paolo shouted at their father.

Reaching the group, she bumped into Vito as he retreated from the fight. His look one of pure rage. "Sorry, princess."

Two hands grabbed her shoulders, looking back, she was relieved to find it was Fernando. Leaning back into his body, she watched her father and his man disappear into the darkness.

Sophia looked over at Paolo. "What happened here?"

Paolo shook his head. "Sorry, Sophia. I didn't mean to start anything."

Sophia walked over to her brother. With a gentle touch, she stroked his cheek. "Are you okay?"

Paolo, with a look of remorse, nodded.

Sophia lifted his chin. "What was that all about?"

Paola looked her straight in the eyes. "Same'o, same'o, Sis."

Sophia looked deep into her dear brother's eyes.

He's not going to tell me anymore.

She kissed his cheek. "Fair enough."

Fernando leaned close to Sophia's ear. "Let's sit for a while before we leave."

Sophia nodded. Linking her arms with Paola and Fernando, the trio went to a nearby table.

CHAPTER THREE

Sophia rolled over to look at the clock on the nightstand. Eight o'clock. Spending a couple of hours with Paolo had made them leave for the mountains later than they had planned. Turning back to the large windows that framed a most spectacular view of the mountains, she snuggled into Fernando's body.

They had arrived after midnight at their honeymoon cabin. Both so tired from all the day's events, they crashed. As much as Sophia wanted to make love, she also wanted more sleep. Closing her eyes, she drifted off.

A soft touch on her ribs aroused Sophia's senses out of sleep. Fernando's hands traveling over her breasts sent tingling sensations to her nipples. Pushing her butt into his manhood, she smiled feeling his readiness.

Turning her face to his cheek, she whispered. "Good morning husband."

Fernando's cheeks wrinkled with his smile. "You are expecting your husband? Then we better make this quick."

Sophia turned in his arms, facing him she poked him in the ribs. "Not this morning. This time will be slow and long."

His sexy smile lit up his mischievous eyes. "As you wish."

The temperature in the room was a bit on the chilly side. The warmth of the heavy quilt made the lovers snuggle down into the softness of the bed. Sophia's eyes adjusted to the dimness. She ran her fingers over the hard muscular chest of Fernando. The joy at finally being his wife, with no one to interrupt or intrude into their world, opened a freedom in her. For once, they had all the time in the world.

She moved her hands over his arms, down to his stomach. If he tried to touch her, she stopped him. "Let me be. I want to explore your body as if it is the first time."

Fernando's smile could be seen in the shadowiness of their cocoon. Allowing her fingers to skim over his body, she felt him relax. Her lips traveled over his skin, licking and probing each inch.

She slipped her hand under his t-shirt. "You have on way too many clothes."

Fernando laughed. "It was cold when we got here last night."

Removing his shirt, she covered his chest with kisses. "Well here, let me warm you up." She felt his body respond to her touch. Kissing his pleasure trail, she untied the sweatpants, slipping them down. Traveling down with her mouth, she removed the unwanted barrier.

She felt his hardness, welcomed the desire rising in her. His groans told her he could not hold back much longer. She straddled his ribs, removed her shirt. His hands cupped her breasts, he pulled her mouth down to his lips. In his kiss she founded all the joy she needed to live a long, and happy life.

His hands removed her pj bottoms as he lifted her up and placed her on his manhood. The rush of him entering her, caused her to explode with a climax too close to the surface. Gripping the sheet under him, she let the ecstasy purge through her. Urging her upward, she let it climb until it crested again.

As he climaxed with her, she closed her eyes, raised her hands, screamed as loud as she could. There was no one to hear, just the two of them. This was the liberation she sought. No longer would there other people to instruct her. It was her and Fernando, just the two of them. When she opened her eyes, he was smiling at her. His hands on her backside, tenderly caressing.

"Oh, Fernando." She slide off of him, rolled to the bed. "We are so blessed."

He raised up, kissing her. "You are free, little one." He drew her to him. "And all mine. No one will ever hurt you again."

Lying together, their naked bodies touching, the warmth of the bed kept them from leaving their bubble.

Sophia traced the line of Fernando's ribs. "Maybe we created a baby."

His chuckle vibrated the bed. "It wasn't for the lack of trying."

Sophia snuggled closer. "I love you. I always have, always will. Nothing you could do will ever make me leave."

Fernando tickled her. "Nothing?"

"Stop! Oh please, you know I hate that!" She was laughing so hard, she had tears.

He ran his hands over her cheek. A deep kiss was his answer. "We will always be together." Sophia kissed him with all the love she had. For there was no one else she loved more in the world.

***

Sophia cooked her first breakfast as a wife. Well, her first meal ever. Even at college, she went to the local coffee shop in the mornings, the student center for lunch, dinner out with friends. She tried, so help her, she tried, but there were so many things to do at the same time. Fortunately, all Giordano men could cook. Without a word, Fernando stepped in and saved the day. Sophia pushed the loose curl of hair from her eyes as she watched him move efficiently from one task from another, fixing her mistakes, adding a gourmet touch to what started out as a simple meal.

As he filled the two plates with his creation, Sophia pour fresh coffee for both of them. Her first pot had been rather strong and bitter. Fernando picked up the two plates, walked over to the breakfast nook. Surrounded by windows, the view of the mountains complimented the now mid-morning breakfast.

Putting the first fork full in her mouth, the taste sensations awakened her hunger. "Wow, I didn't realize how hungry I was."

Fernando nodded. "I don't know about you, but I didn't get a moment to stop to eat yesterday."

Sophia though back. "I think Concetta made me eat breakfast." Lifting another bite to her mouth, Sophia moaned. "How do you know how to cook like this?"

"All the men in my family cook. Uncle Sal is the only one so far to make it as a chef."

Sophia looked over at her new husband. "What shall we do today?"

Fernando wrinkled his forehead. "Well, we could stay in all, day...but...it's a beautiful day. I say we go for a walk, create an appetite for lunch and..." He cocked his head. "...and after."

The implication sparkled in his eyes.

Sophia dabbed her mouth with a napkin. "Why Signor Giordano, I think you are planning to seduce me."

He raised his eyebrows in an evil way. "You are so right."

Fernando gathered up the plates, took them to the kitchen. Sophia followed with the cups and silverware. Working together they cleaned the kitchen. Hand in hand they went upstairs to change into their clothes.

Stepping out into the warm midday sun, they chose to go up the path to the right. Holding her hand, Fernando led her through the trail of brush and loose rocks. Reaching one summit, Sophia looked down into a chasm several hundred feet below. The view made her a bit dizzy.

She grabbed Fernando to hold on to something solid. "That's a long way down."

He wrapped his arms around her. "Stay close."

Again, they followed the path. The incline became steeper, the rocks looser. In her boots, Sophia stepped carefully, feeling very unsure of the ground under her feet. Finally, they reached the crest. Standing together, they looked over the peaks and valleys of the mountain range.

"This is the most spectacular sight I have ever seen." Sophia snuggled her head into the crook of Fernando's shoulder.

Fernando spread out his hand. "It does take your breath away."

As they started back down, Sophia felt her feet move more quickly than she wanted. While it was hard to climb up the trail, coming down was even more treacherous. Suddenly, she found herself too close to the edge. Trying to regain her footing on the rough path, she felt the loose rocks pull her to the edge. Fernando was out of her reach and so was anything else. Then she was falling. Grabbing at air, she screamed as she plunged down the cliff. Hitting a hard surface, she felt a sharp crack as her left leg buckled behind her back. Dazed, she could hear Fernando's voice yelling her name. Trying to focus, she felt him land next to her.

"Sophia!" His voice betrayed his fear. "Talk to me."

Gathering the breath that had been knocked out of her, she spoke low. "I think I broke my leg."

Fernando looked down at her disjointed limb. He took her hand with one of his. "Lay still." He used his cell phone with the other. Speaking in a calm voice, she heard him give directions to where they were.

Hanging up, his words sounded strong, calming. "Help is coming. They said not to move you." His eyes searched her face. "Are you in much pain?"

Sophia didn't know how to answer the question. Everything hurt. She felt the wetness of tears in the corner of her eyes, the first fingers of panic in her chest. So she just nodded.

"Hey, down there?" Both Sophia and Fernando heard the voice at the same time.

Looking up, Sophia saw two men above them with ropes. Fernando squeezed her hand as they watch the men descend down the cliff. Landing on the narrow ledge that had broken Sophia's fall, they handed Fernando the rope.

"They'll pull you up. We'll get her."

Fernando looked back. She could see in his face he didn't want to leave. She gave him a weak smile and nodded.

He turned his back, grabbed the rope and climbed up the rough side avoiding the rocks that jutted out. Sophia kept her eyes on him as the other two men worked on her. After Fernando reached the top, a stretcher was lowered down. Closing her eyes, she fought back the nausea in her throat.

"Ok...what's your name?" One of the men asked.

Opening her eyes, she saw the face of a very kind, but somewhat young looking guy. "Sophia."

"Ok, Sophia." His kind, strong eyes allowed her to trust him. "We are going to lift you up to straighten out your leg. I'm not going to lie. It's going to hurt."

Sophia braced herself.

"Ready?"

She nodded.

In one swift motion, the two men lifted her up. Her left leg was moved back to its right position. The pain shot up her body on both sides to her head. She yelled as a reaction to the god-awful agony.

But then a calm settled over her. She felt safe. That this was under control.

The two men grabbed the sides of the stretcher, lifting her up. Climbing beside her, she felt the stretcher being pulled up the cliff. It was not an easy ride, sharp rocks disturbed the smoothness of the ascent. At times she was upside down. Good thing the straps held her tightly in place.

Finally, she felt the stretcher even out. Opening her eyes, she saw Fernando. She released the breath she had been holding in.

He took her hand, kissed her fingers. "How are you doing?"

Sophia squeezed his hand. No words would come out. She felt a prick in her arm, a fog floating in on her, then nothing.

***

Jerking her eyes open, Sophia's eyes darted around the room. At first her brain did not understand her surroundings. Sterile white walls, blinds closed on the windows. Her gaze stopped when she saw Fernando sitting in the chair to her right. His eyes were shut, his chin resting on his chest.

Sophia tried to moved, but all she could manage was to wiggle her butt. When she tried to lift her head, it felt like a brick was sitting on top. Lying back on the pillows, she felt Fernando come to her side.

His face was drawn with worry. He reached out to touch her, but stopped midway. "How are you?"

Sophia blinked to clear more of the haze. "I don't know."

Fernando swept her hair from her face. "You broke your leg, pretty bad. And you have a slight concussion."

Sophia turned her cheek to fit in his hand. "I am so sorry."

Fernando leaned down to lay a soft kiss on her lips. "For what? Being a klutz is nothing to be sorry for."

He made her laugh, as he always did. "When can I get out of here?"

"Not for twenty-four hours. They want to keep you under observation for your head."

Sophia looked down at her casted leg. She moved it slightly. "And this?"

"Six weeks honey."

"What a way to spend a honeymoon." Sophia looked into the eyes of the man she loved.

He smiled at her. That always present smile that told her it would be all right. "It's a memory maker."

Sophia felt herself getting weepy. "I wanted to make babies." Sobs threatened to explode, she held them back.

Fernando slipped his arm under her back, lowering himself so their chests touched. Kissing her with all the love her felt for her, he whispered against her lips. "We'll have plenty of time for that."

Burying her head in his shoulder, she sucked up the heavenly smell of musk and clean soap.

He's right. We have plenty of time.

Taking his ear lope in her teeth, she whispered. "Can you get me something to eat?"

Laughing, he rubbed his head on her breasts. "I certainly can."

***

Sophia waited very impatiently for the doctor to come in and release her. When he finally walked through the door, her first words were. "I feel great. Can I leave?"

The doctor chuckled. He looked over at Fernando. "She raring and ready to go, isn't she?"

Fernando blushed, looked over at Sophia. "It's our honeymoon."

The doctor smiled, nodded. "I see."

Using his flashlight, Sophia tried to hold still while he looked in her eyes. After checking her head and leg, he nodded. "You can go, but..." he looked over at Fernando. "...keep it low key. Just relax and rest for the next few days. How long are you here for?"

"Just three more days." Fernando looked at Sophia.

The doctor nodded as he wrote on a clipboard. "Fine. Do you have a doctor at home?"

Fernando spoke. "Yes, my cousin is the local doctor."

"Then check in with him." The doctor turned back to Sophia. "Be good. You will heal."

Sophia smiled more for being set free. "I will, I promise."

The doctor took her chart, walked out the door.

Sophia looked over at Fernando, narrowing her eyes, she spoke low and sexy. "Get me out of here."

Fernando held up her clothes. "Way ahead of you, sweetheart."

***

The trip back to the cabin was bumpy and uncomfortable. Sophia didn't complain. She knew Fernando was doing his best. Closing her eyes, she tried to relax, hoping the trip would end soon. Hearing the gravel under the tires and the slowing of the car made her open her eyes to see the welcome sight of their cabin. Fernando came to her side of the car. Opening the door, he knelt down to move her legs out. The heavy cast pulled her forward into his waiting arms.

"Careful honey." Wrapping his arms around her body, he lifted her up and out.

Steadying her, Sophia allowed her head to clear before she tried to take a step.

This is bogus. I have never been so helpless.

Fernando spoke next to her ear as he waited. "It's okay, baby. You will only be helpless for a while."

Nodding, she shifted her weight. "I'm ready. Let's do this."

Together they climbed the two steps to the deck, across the wooden floor to the door. Fernando held it open with his hip, as he manipulated Sophia though. Once inside, he led her to a lounge chair next to the windows. Plopping down, Sophia leaned back into the comfortable cushions and let her breath out.

"You all right?" Fernando leaned down.

Sophia opened her eyes. "Yes, it was just more work than I imagined."

He placed a quick kiss on her forehead. "Rest. I will fix us a lunch."

She chuckled. "Do we have any food?"

Fernando was on his way to the kitchen. "Yes. I had some delivered. We still have two more days here."

Sophia turned her head towards the mountain view in front of her. It was early evening and a mist had settled over the peaks. The retreating sun bathed the landscape a red/orange glaze.

It's nice to have a man that can cook.

***

Since they left the cabin at mid-morning, they arrived at the café by early evening. Pulling in behind the building, Sophia squirmed in her seat.

This leg thing was getting to be a pain.

Looking over the dash, she saw the two familiar motorcycles.

Everyone was here!

As soon as Fernando stopped the car, Sophia pushed open her door.

Running around the back of the car, Fernando shouted at her. "Wait! Don't hurt yourself.

Sophia didn't move. She just took in the fresh smell of the sea. "I just needed some air."

"Okay, but let me help you." Fernando shifted her body so he could grab on to lift her up.

She pushed off from the seat, almost fell on Fernando, but his strong, hard body stopped her action.

"Whoa there. Take it easy." He readjusted his hold. "I've got you."

"I feel so clumsy." Sophia took a break from moving.

Fernando brushed the lose hair from her face. "But you are so cute when you are clumsy."

Good naturedly she smacked him on his chest. "Stop it."

Taking her arm, he allowed her to lean on him as they shuffled to the back door of the café. Sophia straightened up and smoothed down her shirt as Fernando opened the screen door. On her own, she hobbled into the kitchen.

Uncle Sal saw them first. "Sophia. Fernando." He shouted over his shoulder. "They are here." A frown crossed his forehead. "What happened to your foot?"

Before Sophia could answer the whole gang busted through the swinging kitchen doors. First Jessica and Emily, followed by Alejandro and Roberto.

Jessica stopped cold in her tracks. "What the hell happened to you?"

Emily looked shocked at Sophia.

Sophia chuckled. "I fell off a cliff."

Emily stood behind Jessica, looking around her shoulder. "Why?"

Sophia smiled. "It wasn't intentional."

Jessica walked towards Sophia. "Are you in pain?"

"More from embarrassment than injury." Sophia shook her head.

Jessica approached Sophia slowly. Putting her arm gently around her shoulder, she hugged her friend. "Did he push you?"

Laughter pushed out from Sophia's chest. "I don't think so."

The rest of the people in the room joined the laughter. Slapping Fernando on the back, Roberto shouted. "Wine for everyone. Let's toast our newlyweds and the healing of Sophia's leg."

Jessica and Emily both wrapped their arms around Sophia's waist. The strength of both women gave her the balance she needed to move on into the dining room. As soon as they entered, Sophia saw a long table set with flowers, china and many bottles of wine.

Only a few customers remained. They clapped, lifting their glasses as the group moved to the chairs. As the women sat Sophia down, she relaxed into the chair. She decided to ignore the pain of her leg. Anyway, she felt good. Friends and family surrounded her. A hush fell over the room. Sophia looked at the people's faces, then followed their eyes to the dark figure coming through the front door.

He walked over to Sophia, leaned down and kissed her cheek. "Sis. You look beautiful."

"Paolo."

Her brother pulled the chair next to her out. Sitting down he took her hands. "I couldn't miss my sister's homecoming."

Sophia wrapped her arms around his neck. "I am so glad to see you."

He looked down at her foot. "What happened?"

"I got too close to the edge, fell off. Luckily a rock ledge broke my fall and my leg." Sophia shrugged.

Alejandro came up behind her and placed his hands on her shoulders. "Come to the office tomorrow. I'll check it out."

Sophia took her hands out of Paolo's, held them up. "Okay, enough fussing. I am fine. I need food and I

When Dreams Die

need wine." She patted Alejandro's hands on her shoulders and took her brother's hand. "I am good."

***

It was way past midnight when Fernando maneuvered a tired Sophia into their villa. She tried to help, she really did, but too much wine in an already tired body made her pretty useless. Leaning on him, she tried to focus on the journey through the rooms.

Thank god it's only one level.

Using the wall of what seemed like a forever hallway, she felt a surge of relief as they turned the corner to enter the bedroom. As easy as Fernando wanted to be, he kind of dropped her on the bed.

Standing over her, he took deep breaths. "You...o...kay?"

With the room spinning, her body felt no pain. "I'm good. How about you?"

He leaned over her, his arms on both sides. "I will survive." Carefully he untied the strings on her shirt.

She giggled as the feather touch of his fingers tickled her skin. As he lifted her shirt over her head, she felt the cool air touch her bare skin. Goosebumps rose on her arms. Next, she felt his hands on her jeans, pulling the baggie pants from her body. In just her underwear, she snuggled down into the covers, Fernando had turned back. Safe and peaceful, she watched her young, highly sexy husband shed his clothes. Climbing in next to her wearing only his boxers, he gathered her to him.

She whispered to him, as she formed to his body. "Fernando?"

He nudged her neck. "Yes, love."

Wrapping her arms across his. "Do you know I love you more than life itself?"

His voice was soft on her neck. "I do."

"And...?"

His chuckle shook her body slightly. "And you have always been and always will be the love of my life."

The answer gave Sophia the peace she needed to let sleep take over.

CHAPTER FOUR

Sophia woke the next morning to an empty bed and a blazing headache. Feeling across the covers, when she rose up to find Fernando, the pain put her head back on the pillow.

A soft soothing voice whispered in her ear. "Morning love."

Opening her eyes, she touched the smooth face of Fernando. "Is it morning?"

He sat gently down on the bed. "Well, for a couple more hours at least."

Taking a good look at him, her eyes traveled over his crisp look. "Where are you going?"

"To the school. I need to check in. The first semester starts next week."

Sophia moaned. "I need to call my work."

An aged female voice made them both turn towards the doorway. "Knock. Knock." One of the women from the village entered, carrying a tray. "Good morning, Signora Giordano."

Sophia cocked her head and looked at Fernando as he stood. Her question was in her eyes.

He shrugged. "I hired Matas to help you while I am at work."

Sophia let a grin crease her lips. "I'm not helpless."

He leaned down and kissed her. "Of course not. Just a little pampering. Okay?"

"Okay. But I need to be able to do for myself." She again tried to lift her head. The headache stood firm. "Okay maybe today I will let Matas wait on me.

Fernando kissed her with a kiss that could curl her toes. "Good. Rest. Remember you need to see Alejandro sometime today."

Sophia nodded.

Watching him leave, Sophia allowed Matas to arrange the pillows. After being propped up, the tray was placed on her lap. The smell of the coffee enticed her senses. Taking her first sip, she felt the hot liquid work its wonders on her head. The tray was set with buttered toast, a pot of coffee and lots of cream.

Sophia nodded to Matas. "Thank you. This will do good on my swollen head."

Nibbling on her toast, taking another big gulp of coffee, Sophia looked out the oversized French doors to the beautiful sea. It had been the selling point of the villa. The day was bright and beautiful. The slightly open doors wafted in a warm salt water breeze. Relaxing back, she felt like she was returning to being human, she smiled.

Life is good.

***

Matas drove Sophia to Alejandro's office. Alejandro had picked a small comfortable office near the café. As a doctor, he had no desire to be a big shot in the high towers. His love was for the people. So he kept it simple.

She was greeted by an older lady that served as receptionist and nurse. An established Italian, Carmela spoke of the older ways.

"Sophia." Carmela greeted the girl she had known since childhood. Taking a quick glance, she stopped. "What happened?"

Sophia smiled at the all too familiar question "Fell off a cliff." Hobbling her way to the desk. "Does Alejandro have time for me?"

"Sure, anytime."

Sophia searched the near empty waiting room. "Good. I didn't want to interrupt his schedule."

Carmela came around to the front. Taking Sophia's arm, she guided the young girl through the door, down the hallway to an examining room. Helping Sophia onto the table, Carmela walked over to the computer.

She typed quickly as she shot questions. "When did this happen?

"About a week ago."

"How?"

"We were taking a walk and I fell off the edge."

"Ouch. "

Sophia laughed. "You could say that."

Alejandro walked into the room. "I thought I heard you in here." He walked over to Sophia, kissed her cheek. He rotated her casted leg slightly. "Does it hurt much?"

"It's getting better."

He patted her knee. "Rest it. You will be in this for about five more weeks." His eyes narrowed as he looked at her face. "You look tired."

"I am a little. It's been a month. The wedding, this..." she kicked her leg out. "I'm just glad to be settled into our home."

His brown eyes showed the compassion he needed to be a good doctor. "I know. But try to regroup. Take things easier. You have lots of time now."

Sophia was touched by his concern. "Thanks. I think I can now."

Alejandro replaced Carmela at the computer. "Are you working yet?"

"I not for two months." She held her breath waiting for his answer.

"Good." He moved his eyes from the screen to her. "I want to see you back here in four weeks. If it gets really painful, come back immediately." His eyes went back to the screen. "It says you broke it in four places. That's serious."

Sophia looked down at the floor. "I will."

He walked over to her, helped her down. "Call if you need anything. Where's Fernando?"

"He had to check in today."

Alejandro frowned. "How did you get here?"

"Fernando hired a lady."

Alejandro chuckled. "Good for him."

Walking with her to the main door, he handed her off to Matas. "Take good care of her. She is not to do anything strenuous."

Matas nodded. "Si."

As the two tucked Sophia in the car, she waved goodbye to Alejandro as they pulled away.

Matas broke the silence. "You need to get anything?"

Sophia thought. "Yes. Lunch at the café." She wanted to see Jessica. Chit chat woman to woman. Since it was midafternoon, the lunch rush was over. Entering through the back door, Sophia greeted Uncle Sal and Jessica with the elation she felt every time she walked into the warm inviting kitchen.

"Buona sera." Sophia watched the delight reflect on her friend's faces.

Jessica came quickly over to her. "How are you doing?"

"Good. I just saw your husband. He said I would live."

Jessica hugged Sophia. "You look great."

"Funny. Your husband said I looked tired."

Jessica pulled back, studied Sophia's face. "Are you tired?"

"Somewhat, but...you know...everything..." Sophia let go of a pinned in sigh.

Jessica linked her arm through Sophia's. "Come. Sit. Sal will fix you and Matas lunch."

Sophia stopped. "You know Matas?" Pretty sure she had forgotten to introduce them.

"Yes. I'm the one that found her when Fernando called to say he needed someone to help you." Jessica looked back over her shoulder and winked at Matas.

Matas' voice sounded behind Sophia. "I'm going to stay and talk to Salvador. You girls go on and have a girl's lunch."

Pushing on the swinging door, Jessica maneuvered Sophia through to a table. Pulling out a chair, Sophia sat down.

Jessica sat down across from her. Holding Sophia's hands, her voice filled with compassion. "I know what a relief it was for you to leave your father's house. Your brother Paolo has been here several times. It must be nice to reconnect with him."

Sophia squeezed Jessica's hand. "I am so glad he is going to be part of my life. But..." Sophia pursed her lips. "...I feel he is hiding something from me."

Jessica shrugged. "Maybe he is. Give him time. He may open up more. He carries a lot of pain and anger."

Sophia bit her lower lip. "I know. He is very angry at our father."

Jessica patted Sophia's hand then let go to lean back as Josh placed two steaming dishes of pasta in front of them. "Maybe with good reason."

Her words startled Sophia. "Do you know why?"

Jessica shook her head. "Not really." Waving her hands over the food. "Eat. You are too thin." She said in her best Italian voice.

***

The nausea woke Sophia up. She rushed to the bathroom, went down on her knees at the toilet. Not much came up, as last night's supper was light.

Too much wine?
No, actually I didn't drink more than a glass.
The flu?
I don't feel sick anywhere else.

She felt Fernando standing over her. Sitting back on the cold tile, she looked up at him.

"Are you okay?" He sat crossed legged next to her. Putting his arm around her, she laid her head on his shoulder.

Sophia shook her head. "I think so."

Lifting herself up, she walked to the sink to wet a wash cloth. Pressing the coolness to her face, she looked at herself in the mirror. Looking back was a pale face with puffy eyes.

Lifting her gaze, she saw Fernando in the reflection. His forehead was creased with concern.

"I don't think it's anything serious." She wanted to reassure him.

He put his hands gently on her shoulders. "Take it easy today. Maybe it will pass."

Sophia nodded as another wave of nausea broke over her. Going back to her former position at the toilet, she felt the dry heaves shake her body.

For once she wished Fernando wasn't there. Something about throwing up is personal. Between the queasiness, she managed to get out the words. "I'm okay. I'll be down in a minute."

Fernando's voice sounded hurt. "You want me to leave?"

"Yes, please."

"Okay, but if you're not down in ten minutes, I'm coming back up to get up you."

Sophia nodded.

Hearing the door shut, she again sat on the floor, her knees raised, her head on her arms.

Maybe a shower would help.

Crawling over to the stall, she stood slowly, letting her whirling head accept what it was doing. Flipping on the water, she slipped out of her night clothes. The warm water hit her back like tiny love kisses. Letting it fall over her head, she felt her unsettled stomach calm down. As the lost energy resurfaced, she stepped out of the shower and dried her body off. Slipping into a fresh pair of sweats and a tee shirt, she padded into the bedroom. Going to the French doors, she opened them to breath in the fresh morning sea air.

Now I feel better.

Slipping her feet into slippers, she walked down the hall to the kitchen. She was doing okay until the smell of cooking eggs assaulted her nose. Fernando looked up and smiled, then frowned as she put her hand over her mouth and bolted back to the bathroom.

Trying to vomit, she was angry nothing was coming up. Fernando's voice cut through her surge. "Go see Alejandro today, okay?"

Sophia nodded. Then gagged again, gripped the rim and leaned over the bowl.

***

Lying back on the examining table, Sophia felt drained. The weight on her leg threatened to drag her off. Her arm was over her eyes to block the bright light. Hearing the door open and close, she felt a shadow cross over her.

A gentle hand took hold of hers. "Sophia?"

She lowered her arm. "Hi Alejandro."

"So what's happening?"

"I think I got a touch of the flu. I can't keep anything down."

Alejandro pushed on her stomach. She watched his face. He listened to her chest, took her temperature. His look did not give away his feelings.

Finally he nodded. "I want to take some blood tests. Just to see if it's viral or bacterial."

Sophia nodded. He patted her hand. "You'll be okay. Doesn't look like anything serious."

His parting words made her feel better. She didn't need anything else to complicate her life. Her expectations had been met as far as her married life. Waking each morning with Fernando by her side, being the woman of her own house, having good friends and family around to support her, she finally relaxed and enjoyed her days.

Carmela entered the room quietly, stood over Sophia. "Honey I need to take some blood."

Reaching out her hand, Carmela pulled Sophia to a sitting position. "Have a seat in the chair next to the counter."

Sophia was a little light headed as she stepped off the table. Gaining her bearings, she went to the chair. Laying her arm on the cool counter, she turned her head away as Carmela drew the blood. Feeling a bandage being put on her arm, she turned back around.

Carmela patted her arm. "Doctor wants you to give us a urine sample also."

Sophia frowned.

"Nothing to worry about. Just covering bases while he has you here." Carmela's smile convinced Sophia that it was just routine.

Back in the room, swinging her legs while she sat on the table, Sophia's waited with as much patience as she could.

Finally, Alejandro walked into the room. He pulled a rolling stool over, sat down, a file in his hand. "Well, Sophia your nausea is due to you being pregnant." He looked up and smiled.

The words took a while to register, but then Sophia got it. "I'm pregnant?"

Her joy exploded from deep inside of her, bursting out as she shouted. "Are you sure?"

Alejandro laughed. "Pretty sure."

Sophia jumped off the table, almost fell as her cast threw her off balance. Alejandro, pushing off from the stool, caught her.

"Oh my god. This is great! I can't wait to tell Fernando." She stopped and looked at Alejandro. "Don't you tell him."

"I can't, patient slash doctor confidently and all that." His face glowed with his happiness for her. "Plus, this is your moment. What's your plan?"

Sophia stepped back. "Oh...I need to make this special." As she walked away from him she made a mental list. "Dinner, wine...wait wine is no longer an option."

Alejandro put his arm around her shoulder. "Not advisable."

"...okay. No wine, but flowers, candles and..." Her face lit up. "I'll buy a baby outfit." She looked up at him. "Do you know if it's a boy or girl?"

"Little early for that."

She continued. "That's okay."

Together they walked down the hallway. Carmela met them at the waiting room. Matas was sitting in one of the chairs.

Carmela hugged her. "Congratulations."

Matas had a confused look on her face. "Sophia, are you all right?"

Sophia grabbed Matas' arms. "I am better than all right. I'm pregnant." The two women yelled. Sophia's joy was so overwhelming. "Help me plan a special evening to tell Fernando?"

"Of course."

Sophia turned back to Alejandro. "Thank you."

He chuckled. "Don't thank me. Thank Fernando."

CHAPTER FIVE

Sophia and Matas carried the heavy bags into the villa's kitchen. Dropping them on the table, Sophia took a deep breath.

"Do you think we got everything?" Sophia pushed her hair from her eyes.

Matas followed suit and dropped her many bags on the counter. "I can't imagine we forgot anything."

Sophia smiled as she unloaded the groceries.

Tonight will be special.

Her cell phone rang. Looking at the screen, her smile sounded in her voice. "Hello, sweetheart."

Fernando's voice was a welcome sound. "How's my girl?"

"Your girl is great."

"Did you see Alejandro?"

"Yes, it's nothing serious, well nothing bad serious."

"Are you okay?"

Sophia cupped the phone in both hands. "I'm so very okay. What time will you be home?"

"I can come home early..."

"No! I mean not necessary." Sophia looked over at Matas, frowning.

"Well there is a meeting...Is six okay?"

Sophia looked at the clock on the wall. It was three. "Six is fine."

"You get some rest. I'll stop by the café and get dinner."

"No. I mean Matas is fixing dinner. She has already started." Sophia turned to Matas. "That smells good."

"She's already cooking? Are you sure six isn't too late?"

"No...no. She's...building a...sauce. You know how that is?" Sophia's eyes got big as she kept looking at Matas.

"Well, all right. I'll see you around six. Have a good afternoon. Love you."

"Love you too." Sophia ended the call.

"Whew. The man asks a lot of questions." Sophia carried the dry ingredients to the counter.

Matas dumped an arm full of vegetables in the sink. "We will have everything ready. Then I will leave so you can tell your husband the good news."

Sophia smiled as she worked alongside Matas preparing the meal to announce the baby. Reaching up to the radio above her, she tuned in some romantic Italian music. Humming as she worked, she felt so very blessed.

All was fine until the sauce Matas was cooking filtered over to Sophia's nose. Suddenly she was nauseous, scurrying quickly towards the extra bathroom, she reached the toilet just as the dry heaves hit.

How can I throw up? I haven't eaten anything.

Coming out of the small room with a cold, wet cloth, she looked up to see Matas waiting for her.

"Signora. You need to leave the kitchen." Linking her arm through Sophia, she led her to the outside patio to a cushioned lounge in the shade. Sophia didn't protest, she laid down in the cool spot.

Matas came back with some cheese, crackers and a cool clear drink. "You rest. I will finish the cooking."

Sophia took hold of Matas' hand. "Thank you."

Matas chuckled. "My first, I didn't eat for a month."

Sophia felt the wetness in her eyes. "So this is natural? I wanted to have everything perfect..." Tears slipped down her cheeks. "...it has to be a special night."

Matas chuckled. "It will be. You rest. I will fix the meal."

Sophia wiped her cheeks, embarrassed of her crying, but Matas chuckled again. "And the moods, get ready for them."

Sophia leaned back against the cushion.

So many things will change. But all for the good.

Watching the waves silently break across the beach, a feeling of tranquilly caressed her.

***

"Sophia." The quiet voice filtered through her deep sleep. She opened her eyes to see Matas leaning over her. "Sophia, it's five-thirty."

Taking a minute to find her bearings, Sophia blinked. Then the events of the day hit her and she knew why five-thirty was so important. She struggled to sit up. "The dinner?"

"All done."

"Oh, Matas. Thank you so much. You are a life saver." Sophia stood, hugged the woman who now would be her rock for the following months, maybe years.

Matas linked her arm in Sophia's. "Let's get you freshened up to tell Fernando your good news." They reached the hallway.

Hobbling on down the hall, leaning on Matas' arm for support, Sophia's mind went to what to wear. Something soft and sexy. She chuckled.

How sexy can a woman be with a broken leg, who throws up every time she smells food? Oh please get me through this night with some kind of dignity.

Matas helped Sophia into the bathroom. Together they got her seated in the shower, her leg hanging out.

Matas presented the hand held shower head to Sophia. "What do you want to wear?"

Sophia knew the dress. She always wore it when she wanted to feel sexy and desirable. "The ivory colored one."

Matas nodded, left Sophia to enjoy her shower.

As the water fell over her head, Sophia shook her wet hair. Never had she felt so good. Tonight was the beginning of her own life. She rubbed her hand over her still flat stomach.

Little one, you have no idea how much you are wanted.

Finally, her own person. To love and share life with.

Oh, the places they would go. The things they would see.

She didn't care if it was a sweet little girl or a handsome son like Fernando. This child would be loved all the days of its life. Finishing her much welcomed cleanse, Sophia felt revived. Matas appeared at the shower door, holding a large fluffy towel. Sophia grabbed the side of the door, lifted up and into the softness of the fresh smell of the linen.

As Matas wrapped it around her, she hugged its warmth to her. Dragging her heavy leg to the stool, she sat down as she dried off.

"I will be so glad when this thing is off my leg."

Matas took the towel from her, handing over the underwear. "How much longer now?"

"Just one more week."

"You have been good keeping it on."

"Did I have a choice?"

Matas chuckled. "No, but you handled it well."

Sophia stood as Matas dropped the cotton dress over her head. Slipping the straps over her shoulders, she adjusted the bust. Brushing the skirt down, she felt the fabric brush her legs.

Matas pointed to the closet. "Shoes?"

Sophia laughed. "No. Barefoot. What is that saying 'barefoot and pregnant'?"

"Something like that."

They both turned as they heard a car pull into the driveway.

Sophia's excitement overflowed. "He's here."

Matas gently pushed her towards the door. "Go. There are drinks on the patio. I will put the main meal on the table, then go."

Sophia kissed the dear woman's cheek. "Thank you." With as much speed as she could manage, Sophia hurried down the hall reaching the door just as Fernando opened it.

He took one long glance down her body. "I see you are wearing 'the dress'. "

Sophia nestled into his arms, burrowing her nose in his chest to gather the sweet, manly smell of him. "You know me too well."

His hug told her she was in the arms of her only love.

Well until now.

Wrapping her arm around his waist, she guided him to the patio. On the bar sat two glasses and two bottles. One with wine, the other a non-alcoholic drink.

Fernando frowned. "What is this?"

Sophia handed the glass of wine to him. Lifted her glass and clinked against his. "For me and..." She paused for affect. "...and the baby we are going to have."

Fernando's look was first surprise, then pure joy exploded over her his face. "Are you serious?"

Sophia nodded. "Yes, Alejandro ran the test. What I have is morning sickness. Well more morning, noon and night sickness..."

Before she could finish her sentence, he swept her into his arms and kissed her. A deep, passionate kiss that symbolized the love they had for each other.

"I can't believe it. How? When?"

Sophia placed her hands on his chest. "I think you know how. When? I'm guessing our wedding night, since we haven't make love since." She searched his face. His joy illuminated.

Biting her lower lip, she tilted her head. "Can you believe? We are going to be parents."

Fernando hugged her, resting his chin on her head. "I can believe it."

Sophia laid her head on his chest. Her safe place, always had been since they were kids. Looking up, she kissed his cheek. "Let's eat. Matas has fixed us a fantastic meal."

Arm in arm they walked into the dining room. The table was set with the good china. Candles and white gardenias graced the center. Fernando pulled out her chair, then sat across from her.

Lifting off the covering together, as soon as the delicious smell filtered up, Sophia felt the churning in her stomach. Grabbing the cloth napkin, she rushed to the bathroom. Down on her knees, grabbing the rim of the toilet, she felt Fernando behind her.

"So we do this for nine months?'

"What's this 'we' shit?" Sophia was getting tired all ready of not being able to eat. She was hungry. Finally, the heaves quit. She turned and sat on the cold floor. Fernando handed her a cold, wet cloth.

Sitting down next to her, he took her hand. "I'm sorry. This has to be uncomfortable for you." She could tell by his tone her was trying not to laugh.

She smacked him on the arm. "You think?"

Rubbing his arm, he laughed out loud. "I am just so overjoyed that we are going to have a baby."

Sophia took his arm and wrapped it around her shoulder. Leaning against his side she smiled. "I am too. No matter what it takes, I am so happy to be carrying our child."

Fernando kissed the top of her head. "Me too."

***

When Dreams Die

Sophia stood behind Fernando as he opened their villa's door. Jessica stood in front of the whole gang.

Holding up a bottle of wine, Jessica gave an Italian yelp. "Ciao! We're here for the party."

Swooping pass Fernando, Jessica hugged Sophia. "What are we celebrating?"

Sophia avoided the question. "Can't we just celebrate getting together?"

Emily came up behind the two. "Yes we can. Let's celebrate life."

Sophia bit her lower lip.

You don't know how close to the truth you are.

The three women walked arm in arm outside. The evening colors blanketing the horizon, reflecting on the water. The glow of the sparking lights surrounding the veranda gave the night a magical feel.

As the men filtered in, Fernando poured a glass of Jessica's wine for everyone except Sophia. For her he discreetly had a glass of non-alcoholic sparkling juice. Putting the flutes on a tray, he handed Sophia hers. Passing out the rest, the first thing Roberto did was swirl the sparkling gold liquid, then raised it to his nose.

"Sweet. Expensive."

The others turned their heads to look at Sophia and Fernando.

Jessica frowned. "What's the occasion?"

Fernando drew Sophia to his side. She looked at the faces of her dear friends.

Lifting his glass, Fernando announced. "We...Sophia and I are pleased to announced that we are having a baby."

Each face portrayed a different expression. Jessica's and Emily's looks were pure joy.

"Oh, Sophia!" Jessica went to hug her.

Emily followed. "I am so glad for you."

Roberto slapped Fernando on the back. "Son of gun."

Alejandro stood back, nodded to Fernando.

Jessica talked a mile a minute. "You've seen a...doctor..." She narrowed her eyes, turned around to glare at Alejandro. "You knew? And didn't tell me?"

Alejandro raised his hands in defense. "Patient stash doctor privilege."

Jessica gave him a smothering look. "Okay. I guess." She lifted her glass. "Let's do this again. To Sophia and Fernando and their baby."

Everyone clinked their glasses. As Sophia started to take a sip, Jessica stopped her. "You can't drink. Fernando what are you thinking?"

Fernando chuckled. "Way ahead of you Jess. Non-alcoholic."

She patted his cheek. "Good boy. You'll do as a father."

Together they all raised their glasses to the joyful event about to happen to their friends.

Dinner was a buffet set up at the end of the terrace. As they finished, the three women sat together in the large swing that overlooked the sea.

Sophia felt her emotions rising. "Thank you all for being with me for this."

Jessica sighed. "Wouldn't want to be anywhere else."

Sophia took hold of Emily's hand. "What about you? Any plans?"

Emily smiled. "Not official, but I think this thing between me and Roberto is going to work out."

Jessica leaned forward to look at Emily. "That's a pretty indefinite definite."

Emily leaned back. "Time. Time will tell."

"Speaking of time..." Jessica turned her attention to Sophia. "Have you told Paola?"

"Tomorrow. I am meeting him for lunch."

Jessica pressed on. "And your father?"

Sophia shook her head. "No. We are going to Bella's in a couple of weeks to tell all of them. I will tell him then."

Jessica took Sophia's hand, squeezed it. "It'll be alright."

Sophia felt a deep sadness come over her. Looking out over the beauty of the night, she only wanted to think good thoughts for her baby. "It doesn't matter. I am doing what I have waited years for. I am married to the man I love and we are having a baby. I will cherish this child."

Both Jessica and Emily held Sophia's hand, rocking back and forth in the silence of the night.

CHAPTER SIX

Sophia took a sip of her water, munched on another bread stick while waiting for Paola. He wasn't really late, she just arrived early. Why she was nervous, she didn't know. Telling her brother was not going to be the hard part. Telling her father would be. A hand touched her shoulder. She looked up into the kind eyes of her dear brother. He kissed her cheek.

"Am I late?" He sat down on the chair across from her. He looked at the empty bread basket.

Sophia shook her head as her mouth was full. Her morning sickness had ceased for now and she found she was always hungry. Making up for lost time, she guessed.

Paola motioned for the waiter. As the young lady approached, he asked Sophia. "What kind of wine?"

"None, thank you."

He frowned. "Are you all right?" His attention went to his sister, ignoring the girl waiting for his order.

Sophia looked up apologetically. "Yes, I'm fine. Order your wine. The waitress is waiting."

Paola didn't take his eyes off of Sophia. "Your house red."

"Very good sir." The girl looked to Sophia.

When Dreams Die

"Just water is fine."

Paola took Sophia's hands, his eyes deep with worry. "Okay spill. What's going on?"

Sophia wanted it to be a special announcement, but... "I'm pregnant."

Paola's face lit up, he squeezed her hands. "Seriously?" He leaned back in his chair. "I'm going to be an uncle."

"A spoil them rotten uncle?" Sophia never knew how her brother felt about kids.

"Of course. Is it too soon to buy a pony?" A smile twitched at the corners of his mouth.

The relief and gladness encompassed Sophia. "Probably."

He nodded his head. "So that's why no wine."

"Yes, but food, now food I can't get enough of." Sophia joked with him.

"Then let's order." Releasing her hands, he picked up the empty basket. "I see you've taken pretty good care of these."

The waitress placed Paola's glass of wine down. Paola looked at her for the first time. "We'll start with the house salad, then the daily special. We'll let you know about dessert."

The young girl, now finally satisfied that she had the handsome man's attention. "And your wife?"

Paola knew the ploy. "Not my wife." He looked across at Sophia. "My very dear pregnant sister."

Sophia could almost hear the girl's silent sigh. "Very good."

As she left, Sophia kicked Paola under the table. "You dog. She was flirting with you."

Paola shrugged. "I know. Any other time I would have played the game. But today is about you and your good news." His face took on a solemn look. "Have you told father?"

Sophia paused, took in Paola's expression. He looked uncomfortable. "No."

His tone had a sharp edge. "Are you planning to?"

Nodding, Sophia knew she dreaded the thought of facing her father again. "Yes. We are going to Bella's next week. I will tell him then."

Paola angled his head, but his eyes stayed on her. "Are you afraid?"

Sophia pushed her hair from her face. "No, it isn't fear. It's…I don't want him to dampen this glorious thing."

"You do know he will never be the doting grandfather." He sneered.

"I do know. He wasn't the doting father." Her bitterness surfaced. "If I had my way he wouldn't know or ever see the baby."

"I can understand, but that's not you. You play fair. And the right thing to do is tell him. Just remember how he reacts is not your problem, it's his."

"Tell me, if you were having a baby, would you tell him?" Sophia always wondered if Paola married, would he think differently towards their father.

Paola hesitated. "No. For me it's none of his business."

The server set the salads in front of them. Sophia took her napkin, unfolded it and placed it in her lap. She didn't want to talk about their father anymore. She wanted to enjoy this precious time with her brother.

Before she took a bite, she laid the bombshell on him. "Any new women in your life?"

Paola grinned. "Women? Plural?" He winked at her. "Not yet. But seeing you and Fernando makes me think I could do this marriage thing."

"I think you would make a good husband. And a great father. Think about it, brother. You deserve to have all life has to offer."

"Do I? It seems I just get by." Paola words showed the first crack Sophia had ever seen in his hard shell.

"That's because you bury your feelings. Open up to love." She waved her fork in the air.

Paola mocked her. "Love. What I've seen, it's not always good."

"But it can be." Sophia felt such sadness for her brother. She knew he had seen the worst of their parent's marriage. "I love you."

Paola paused. He was taken aback by her words. But she could see in his eyes he believed her.

The words came hard, she knew. But he said them. "You are the only person in this world that I do love."

She raised her water glass. "It's a start."

***

Sophia adjusted her proper business attire. Pushing against the heavy glass door, the butterflies in her stomach would not calm down. Today she was going to see her new workplace and the second half of Tomei and Calabria. Mr. Tomei had been the one to interview her. Now it was Mr. Calabria she needed to impress.

Limping up to the reception desk, she took a deep breath. "I'm here to see Mr. Calabria."

The young girl smiled. "It's Ms."

Sophia felt foolish.

How could I not know that?

She had researched the company. For some reason she thought the owners were both men.

Sophia gave the girl a smile. "Thanks for the heads up."

The girl laughed. "It's a common mistake. I think Ms. Calabria does it on purpose. I usually let the men walk in cold, but you are one of us. We girls stick together."

I like her.

Sophia smiled. "I owe you one."

The girl stood up. She was sharply dressed in a fashionable suit. "I'm Telica. Come this way."

As she rounded the large desk, she noticed the leg brace. "On my! What did you do?"

Sophia chuckled. After tomorrow she wouldn't have to explain. "I fell off of a cliff."

As the two women walked down the hallway, Telica's eyes got big. "Ouch."

Sophia hobbled down the hall trying to keep up. "Pretty much."

They stopped in front of a large wooden door. Telica knocked, then pushed the door open. "Ms Calabria, Sophia Rossi is here to see you."

A tall slender, 'take no prisoners' stylist woman stood. "Ms Rossi."

Sophia felt Telica leave behind her, the click of the door. Standing straight, she walked to the desk, held out her hand. "It's Mrs. Giordano now. I got married."

Ms Calabria's look went to Sophia's foot. "And broke your leg?"

Sophia felt a blush start on her cheeks. "Yes."

Ms Calabria waved her hand to the chairs in front of her chic glass desk. "Sit."

Sophia glanced at the name plate as she sat down.

Jayme Calabria. That was it. She was listed as Jay Calabria.

Jayme sat down, looked at the papers in front of her. As if talking to herself she repeated Sophia's information. "Grew-up in the wine region. Graduated top of your class." She looked over her glasses. "Won first place in the national design contest." Removing her glasses, she leaned back in her chair. "I can see why Calvino hired you."

Sophia sat speechless. The opening of the door broke the silence. Calvino Tomei walked in, went straight to Sophia.

The sight of her leg stopped him. "What happened?"

Sophia looked back and forth between the two. "I fell off a cliff on my honeymoon."

Calvino frowned. Jayme snickered.

"'I'm fine, really. I get it off in two days. The brace not the leg." She didn't know why she was babbling. "I am just so excited to start work..." she stopped mid-sentence. Took a breath.

Calvino took the chair next to Sophia, patted her arm. "It's fine. You look good..."

Sophia twisted her hands. "I need to tell you...I just found out I'm pregnant."

While she expected shock, instead she got approving looks from both.

Jayme looked to Calvino. "Well, I think we can work with that."

Sophia let out a silent sigh. "Thank you."

Calvino and Jayme stood, so Sophia followed suit. *Guess the interview's over.*

As Jayme came around the desk, Calvino held out his arm. "Let's go look at your office."

My office. What a sweet sound.

Taking his arm, Sophia looked at Jayme standing by the door.

"Sophia, it's been a pleasure to meet you. Broken leg, baby and all. See you in two weeks."

Sophia liked Jayme. While she seemed hard-core, she was a nice person. "Thank you. I am ready to work."

"Just take care. We want a healthy baby and mother." She turned her look to Calvino. "Show her our little company here."

As Calvino and Sophia left the office, he took her down the hallway. At one door, he turned. As they walked in, Sophia gasped. The office was huge with modern furnishings, a whole wall of windows that looked over the sparkling blue sea.

"Oh, Mr. Tomei. This is beautiful." She released his arm and moved to the windows. Turning back around, she saw the work station that covered one whole wall. Everything an architect needed.

"Call me Calvino." He moved to the computer. "Everything is state of the art. But the software is also transportable, so you can access it at home. So on the days you don't feel well, you can work from home."

The words surprised Sophia. "Really?" She had not expected them to be so accommodating.

"We don't care where you work as long as the work gets done." He chuckled. "You can go sit on the beach if you want." He picked up a bag. "Here's a laptop. Take it home. Get familiar with it. Then you'll be ready to go."

Sophia took the bag, swung it over her shoulder. "I will be ready." She hated to leave her new office, but she knew Calvino was busy. Going back out into the hallway, she shook his hand. "Thank you so much. I won't disappoint you, I promise."

Calvino covered her hand with his other one. "I know you won't. That's why I picked you."

Grinning she turned and hobbled down the hall. Glancing in the other offices, she saw people busy.

I like this place.

Coming to the front desk, Telica looked up as Sophia approached. Sophia leaned on the edge of the desk. "Telica, you were a life saver. Thank you."

Telica smiled. "It's good to have you."

Sophia walked to the elevators, hit the down button. She felt good. Things were working out quite well, as she had always dreamed. In the empty elevator, she rested against the back wall. She relaxed as the car passed by three floors. At "L" the doors opened. Sophia went to the bright, sunny outside. Her workplace was in the heart of the village's business district. Since it was such a nice day, she decided to explore her surroundings. The street level of the alleyway was lined with shops of all kinds. Checking them out, she noticed the name *Giordano*.

Uncle Lucca?

She pushed against the glass door, heard the bell ring. Stopping mid-opening, she looked at the woman that looked up from the desk.

"Emily!" Sophia was surprised to see her. "You work here?"

Emily jumped up and hurried around the desk. "Sophia! What are you doing here?"

Sophia let the door shut behind her. "I was checking in with my work. Uncle Lucca's office?"

A male voice sounded as Lucca passed through his office door. "It sure is. Sophia, so good to see you." Lucca had been a part of Sophia's life forever. She remembered when his wife died. If she remembered right it was close to when her mother left. He crossed the room and pulled her into a big hug. She returned the deep affection she had for him.

As they parted, he looked into her eyes. "You are glowing."

Sophia blushed, looking over his shoulder at Emily. "I'm pregnant."

Lucca's face lit up. "Oh wow! How great! When? What is it?"

She shook her head. "In the end of winter around February. We don't know yet what it is."

Lucca's smile took over his whole face. "I am so happy for you two." He turned to Emily. "I say we close the office and go to our favorite café to celebrate."

Emily shut his office door. "Way ahead of you, boss." Keys jangled in her hand. The three walked out.

Lucca looked down at Sophia's foot. "Can you walk there?"

Sophia linked her arms with him and Emily. "Yes, I can. Just hold me up."

The three took off down the winding path to the sea's edge. Greeted at the back door by Jessica and Uncle Sal. One of the ladies asked about Matas.

Sophia knew she was a cousin. "I gave her the day off. I only have two more days with this contraption on my leg."

Uncle Sal hugged Sophia. "I hear good blessings are in order."

"Oh, Uncle Sal, we are so thrilled."

"Well you better get to Bella's soon. The word has leaked out. She and Gina are chomping at the bit to see you."

"This weekend. I think everyone is coming."

Jessica took Sophia's arm, reached back for Emily. "Yes, we all our coming. Even Roberto and Emily."

Sophia looked around Jessica to Emily. "How awesome. Do you see him much?"

Emily shrugged. "Enough. He's busy doing what he loves. I'm good."

As they sat down, Sophia looked over at Emily. "Don't you miss him?"

Emily looked down at the table, paused. "Terribly. But having him sometimes is better than no times."

Sophia nodded. The Giordano men each had their own charm. And the women they loved were secure with that.

Uncle Sal and Lucca joined the girls' table. Bringing wine and sparkling juice, Uncle Sal poured the glasses full and Lucca made a toast. "To the women of the Giordano men. Love much."

Raising their glasses each toasted, clinked and drank. Then the kitchen staff brought the food.

***

Sophia rolled over in bed to reach for Fernando. The lack of heavy weight on her leg still surprised her. Finding his body, she wrapped both of her legs around his.

He stirred, ran his hand over her side. "You feel good."

She licked his back. "You feel better. Plus you taste good."

He rolled over to face her. Pushing her hair out of her face, he kissed her nose. "Do we have time?"

She nestled into his body. "We always have time."

"Matas?"

"Not here today." She climbed up on him. "We are alone."

Running his hands over her butt, he leaned up and kissed her breasts. "Let's do it."

"So romantic." She jested with him.

He smiled. "Do you want romance or great sex?"

She knew the answer, but paused as if she were pondering. "Both. I want both."

Flipping her on her back, he kissed her deep. "You got it."

His mouth did wonders to her senses. It had been too long and her body responded quickly. But Fernando, a master at prolonging her climax, teased her unmercifully. She gripped his hair as his mouth traveled down her body. Twisting, she could feel the tip of the peak he was bringing her to. She wanted to claw at his back, bring him inside of her. He continued his downward travels. Each spot his tongue touched became hot. Her whole body wanted him. She wanted to beg, but then again not. The longer the anticipation, the greater the thrill.

Her love for this man never ceased to amaze her. Each time they made love it grew stronger. And now that they had made a child she felt they were totally one.

She jerked as he touched the spot with his tongue. Probing, each lick brought a heightened wave. She felt it build, just short of the crest.

Leaving her on the cliff, he came up and kissed her. Then he entered her. Her emotions took over as she cried out. Feeling his body shake, she crested with him. The sweat on her breasts mingled with his. Drops fell from his hair. One landed on her lips. She sucked in the salty taste.

As he rolled off, she nestled in his side. "Dear husband, I love you so much."

She could feel his smile. "Dear wife, I love you more."

She wanted to reply

No you don't.

But it didn't matter. They loved each more than anyone else and that's all that mattered.

CHAPTER SEVEN

Getting into Fernando's car, Sophia had a thought. "You know we need a different car for the baby. I don't think the Maserati is practical and this is..." she had to be careful. Fernando loved his little bright yellow Fiat. "...small."

Fernando looked over at her. "I like the sound of that."

Sophia frowned. "A new car?"

"No 'the baby'." He took her hand. "It's real isn't it?"

Sophia rubbed her starting to bulge stomach. "Yes, it is."

Starting the car, Fernando continued the conversation. "So what do we want? A nice sedan? A minivan? Or..." He wrinkled his nose. "A station wagon?"

Laughing, Sophia looked over at him. "I don't think they make station wagons anymore. A minivan is a little much. How about just a nice utility vehicle? Fiat makes one."

"What color?" His question was totally serious.

Sophia patted his hand. "Whatever you want, honey."

"You've been thinking about this for a while."

"I have been thinking about everything for the baby." Sophia leaned back. Her thoughts these days were of nothing else.

They were driving to Bella's. The family was gathering for the wine harvest celebration. It was an event celebrated every year. This year would be special. Sophia was anxious to see Fernando's family. While the good news had leaked out, she still wanted to show them how happy she and Fernando were.

The hour drive seemed quicker. But then, Sophia was in her own world. Talking non-stop they discussed baby names, furniture and their future.

As they pulled into the driveway, Sophia sat up right. No sooner had Fernando stopped the car, than Bella, Orlinda and Gina came bouncing down the steps.

Sophia opened her door the same time Bella grabbed the handle. "Sophia!" Bella scooped her up in a hug.

Orlinda was jumping up and down. Finally Bella released her and Orlinda took her into another hug. "I am going to be a grandma."

Gina hugged her last. "We are so happy for you."

Sophia looked over her shoulder at Fernando. He was standing with his father, beaming. She winked at him as she was drug into the house. The three women walked on through the villa to the outside. On the terrace sat Jessica and Emily. Three chairs sat waiting. As soon as Sophia sat down a mug of hot apple cider was sat in front of her. A plate of pepsakoy, an Italian almond and orange cookie, sat in the middle of the table. She grabbed one, let the sweet taste melt in her mouth.

Leaning back, she sighed. Being here on the sparkling fall day felt so good. Bella's had been her second home. This had been her safe place, still was.

Bella sat on her right. "Are you all right?"

Sophia beamed. "Yes. I am great."

Orlinda was on her left. "How is the pregnancy going?"

Sophia patted her mother-in-law's hand. "Good. Had a lot of morning sickness, but that seems to have passed."

"Your foot?" Orlinda looked down.

Sophia instinctively kicked it out. "The cast is off and it's fine."

Bella looked over at Jessica and Emily. "Now I trust you girls are taking care of our little Sophia." Her tone was commanding as usually.

Jessica saluted. "Yes, ma'am. We are on it." The jesting lighten the mood.

Bella shook her head. "You girls." She narrowed her look at Emily. "And when are you and my grandson going to get married?"

Before the stunned Emily could speak, Gina piped up. "Mama. Leave her alone. They will in their own time."

"Ump. Their own time." Bella waved her hand. "What time? They love each other. What are they waiting for?"

Emily opened her mouth to speak, but Gina's words were out first. "They are very busy. When Roberto decides to stay on this continent, then they will get married, have babies." She turned to Emily. "Right?"

Jessica nudged Emily in the ribs, whispered. "Just say yes."

Emily looked at Gina and Bella with her best innocent look. "Yes."

Sophia, Jessica and Emily hid their snickers. Bella was somewhat satisfied. Gina, pleased she had won this battle.

Before she could stop it, Sophia yawned. "I'm sorry. It seems I am always tired these days."

Gina patted her arm. "Don't apologize. You go up and take a nap. You need your rest."

It sounded like a good idea. "Excuse me, will you?" She stood.

All echoed. "Of course."

Sophia turned to look for Fernando. Standing with the men, she caught his eye. He frowned. She mouthed. "Going upstairs."

He started to move towards her. She held up her hand. "No. I'm fine. Stay."

He furrowed his forehead. "You sure?"

Sophia blew him a kiss. "Yes. Love you."

His smile warmed her heart as it always did. "Love you too."

Sophia went back into villa, slowly climbing the staircase. Going to their usual room, she opened the door to the huge bedroom. The French doors were wide open allowing the chilly sea breeze to cool the room. She went over to close them, taking a long glance at the crystal blue sea and her father's house.

Tomorrow. I will go see him tomorrow.

Crawling under the quilt, she let sleep take over.
Tomorrow

***

Light kisses on her cheek woke Sophia slowly. Before she opened her eyes, she breathed in the sweet smell of her husband.

She moaned as she stretched out her legs, taking a moment to open her eyes. The tickling of her ribs made her blink.

Laughing, she grabbed his arms. "Stop!"

He obeyed her, scooping her into his arms. "How do you feel?"

"I feel fine." She stretched her arms over her head. "What time is it?"

"Dinner time. Hungry?"

"Always." She let him pull her up to a sitting position. "Give me a minute."

He helped her the rest of way out of the bed. Bending to kiss her belly, she ran her fingers through his hair.

When he straightened up, she could see the love in his eyes. Rubbing her stomach, she smiled at him. "It's real. I promise."

He spoke against her skin. "I can't wait to have you and 'it' as my family."

"You have us now." She stroked his hair.

He raised up, took her in his arms. "I know. Sometimes it feels surreal, like I'm waiting for the bubble to pop."

"It won't pop." She rubbed her belly again. "It will just get bigger."

He bent to kiss it again. "Ready for you little one."

"Well, the little one needs to get ready." Sophia moved to the bathroom.

Fernando spoke to her back. "When are you going to tell your father?"

Sophia stopped at the door. "Tomorrow."

"All right. I am going with you."

Her love for him fell over her in soft waves. She turned to look back at him. "Thank you."

Fernando stood in the middle of the room and shrugged. "It's where I need to be.

***

The evening festivities were simple and relaxed. Dinner prepared by the top cooks in the family. Since the evening turned cool at sundown, the large dining room was filled to brimming. Sophia sat next to Fernando, the many aunt, uncles and cousins lined the table. Bella was naturally at the head, Marcello at the other end. The feast was overwhelming. Too much food as always.

Sophia's stomach growled. She patted her belly, sending silent messages to the baby.

Quiet, little one. You'll embarrass me. I'm eating as fast as I can.

Digging into the first course, the bruschetta woke her taste buds and quieted her stomach. The normal table chatter rose to a high noise level. The men argued about sports. The women discussed fashion and gossip. As the male voices became loud, the female matched the pitch. So it sounded like everyone was shouting in both Italian and English. Sophia chuckled to herself. She so loved this. Her child would grow up with a huge family and many such dinners. Not like the quiet meals she ate alone.

As the many courses crossed in front of her, Sophia finally got her fill. As people started leaving the table, the older women cleared the dishes. The young girls were not yet invited into the kitchen. At what age, Sophia did not know, but her time would come.

Weaving through the crowd, she found her way outside to the terrace. Leaning on the rail, she wished she had grabbed a coat. The forecast predicated a fall frost for the night. Nothing heavy, but enough to mark the end of the grape growing season. A warm wrap on her shoulders, made her smile.

"I figured you would be cold out here." Fernando kissed her cheek.

She hugged the warm shawl around her. "You are right."

His voice carried a hint of anxiety. "You okay?"

She leaned back against him. "Yes just needed some air."

The full moon was on its way to the center of the night sky. Sophia looked over the only place she had ever known as a child.

Being a mother must bring up memories of my life as a child.

Fernando leaned on the banister next to her. "Yes, they can be quite overwhelming, my family."

Sophia shook her head. "You forget I spent lots of time over here." She looked over at him. "I would sneak over here on holidays because I didn't want to be alone."

She could see his amazing smile even in the darkness. "And here I thought it was to see me."

She laid her head on his shoulder. "It was. I didn't like days that I didn't see you."

"Well, those days are behind you. You will see me every day for the rest of your life."

"And after." Sophia raised her head, frowning. The words seemed to come out for no reason.

Fernando stood back. "And after? I thought all I agreed to was 'til death do us part'.

She lightly fisted him in his ribs. "Wrong bucko. Forever. You are stuck with me forever."

He nodded. "I can handle that."

She put her head back on his shoulder, her arm around his waist. "Good because it is non-negotiable."

He kissed the top of head. "I can live with that."

***

Sophia pulled her favorite worn jeans over her hips. Feeling the tightness in the waist, she was glad they were a bit baggy. Slipping the heavy sweater over her head, as she pushed her arms through the sleeves, she walked to the big window. A heavy fog rolled in. She couldn't see the beach. Pulling the bottom of her sweater down, she sat on the bed, pulling on her sneakers.

Fernando waited downstairs for her. They were going to walk over together to see her father. Sophia placed her hands on her knees and stretched.

Let's do this.

Leaving the bedroom, she bounced down the stairs. She refused to let this ruin her good feeling. Her father would just be told the news. How he reacted was not her problem or concern. Her days of walking on egg shells to avoid a confrontation with him were over.

This is how it is.

Walking into the kitchen she found many people milling around. Spotting Fernando at the counter, she slipped up behind him, circled his waist with her arms.

"Good morning, husband."

He leaned back into her. "Good morning wife. Sleep well?"

"Always." She lifted up onto the stool next to his.

Orlinda set a cup of coffee in front of her. "So what are your plans for today, kids?"

Taking her first sip, she felt the invigorating liquid slide down her throat. "We're going over to tell my father the news about the baby."

The distress on Orlinda's face was obvious. "How do you think he will take it?"

Sophia shrugged. "Doesn't matter. It's a good thing whether he likes it or not."

Orlinda patted Sophia's hand. "How could he not."

Ever since Sophia's mother left, the Giordano women had stood in for her. Each of them offered a part, so in reality she had a whole mother, just not in one person. A plate of breakfast food was placed in front of Sophia. Looking up she smiled at Bella.

The stern woman's face foretold her words. "He will accept your news with his normal reserve. Don't expect any big display of emotions."

With her mouth full of food, Sophia shook her head. Taking a gulp of coffee she could finally could speak. "I don't." She took Fernando's hand. "Fernando will be there with me."

When Dreams Die

Bella stroked her grandson's face. "Take care of her, as you always have."

Fernando patted Sophia's hand. "You know I will."

***

By the time they started their walk to the Rossi villa, the sun had burned off most of the fog. It promised to be a nice day. Sophia hoped so. The women always did a traditional grape stomping ceremony for harvest. While modern technology had improved the wine making progress, the old ways were still honored.

Stepping over the stones and shells, when they got to the rugged rocks that separated the two properties, Fernando, lifted Sophia up to the flat top. Sophia smiled at the memories of sitting there waiting for Fernando.

As they came to the path from the house, Sophia felt her stomach jump.

Steady child. This will be over soon.

Entering through the kitchen, Sophia put her finger to her mouth, signaling for Fernando to be quiet. Concetta stood at the sink with her back to the door.

Sophia tiptoed behind her. Circling Concetta's shoulders with her arms. "Hey lady."

Concetta dropped her knife. Turned around and took Sophia into a big hug. "Child." She reached out her hand to Fernando. "Come here."

Hugging them both, they could hear the happiness in her voice.

Sophia pulled back first. "Is father here?"

"Yes, he is in the library."

Sophia took in the aroma of garlic and herbs. "What are you cooking?"

Concetta released them both, turned to look at the sink. "Nothing. I hardly cook at all. The Signor is hardly ever here." Her face lit up. "I can fix you something!"

Sophia chuckled. "No. We just ate. But I wouldn't say no to a cup of your fabulous coffee. Maybe some biscotti?" She rubbed her stomach. "I am eating for two now."

Concetta erupted into glee. "Oh, my. How exciting!" Again with the hugs for both of them.

Concetta waved them on. "Go. Find your father. I will bring in the coffee and biscotti."

Sophia hugged her back. "Thank you." Taking Fernando's hand she led him to the library.

Knocking lightly on the heavy wooden door, she quietly spoke. "Papa?" She heard the scraping of the chair on the wooden floor.

The door opened. Vito stood back as they entered. Sophia looked around. "Where are your men?"

Vito stammered. "I didn't need them today." He motioned to the sitting area of rich, overstuffed, leather furniture. Sophia, still holding Fernando's hand walked over to the couch. As they sat down, Vito took the chair.

The silence hung like the morning fog in the room.

"So papa..."

"Sophia...

They both spoke at the same time.

Vito bowed, nodded to her.

Sophia squeezed Fernando's hand, sat up straight. "So...Papa, how have you been?" She didn't want to just drop a bombshell on her father.

Let's ease into this.

Vito leaned back. "I've been good. Busy. The wine business is growing..." His voice trailed off. His sad eyes looked at her. "You?"

Sophia smiled. "Well, I...We have some good news."

Here goes nothing.

"We are expecting a baby."

Vito's look didn't change. "A baby..." He said softly, letting his voice trail off. Snapping back. "That's good news."

"Really?" Sophia felt the hint of gladness rise in her chest.

Vito frowned. "Aren't you happy about it?"

Sophia took a deep breath. "Yes. I just didn't know how you would take it."

He shrugged. "I am fine with it. I have been expecting it." His face softened. "You always wanted to be a mother ever since..."

Concetta interrupted. Sitting a tray of coffee and cookies on the coffee table, she smiled at everyone, unaware she had stopped a conversation.

Her face was beaming. She raised her eyebrows at Sophia.

Sophia nodded.

Concetta finished pouring the coffee, retreated from the room.

Sophia turned to her father. "So you feel like being a grandfather?"

Vito shrugged. "I guess. Does it matter?"

Sophia felt the crush of his empty words. "No, it doesn't." She went silent, her mind wandered to how she had set herself up for the disappointment of her father's reaction. She needed to get out of here. The place that was her home now depressed and suffocated her.

She stood, looking down at Fernando. "We need to go. The festivities will start soon." Fernando read her face as he always did. No questions or objection, he rose also.

Vito came out of his chair with a slight bit of difficultly. Sophia noticed his slower movements, the aging of his face, the graying of his hair.

You are going to grow old by yourself, ole' man. And you did it.

The fact she had no empathy for him troubled her, but she shook off the guilt.

It is what it is.

As she started for the door, Vito stopped her. In a surprised move, he hugged her. Not his normal distance hug, but a real feeling hug.

He whispered in her ear. "Be happy, princess."

The tears threatened to fall, but she fought them back. When he pulled back, she saw the wetness in his eyes. This was a side of her father she had never seen.

Were there regrets in her father's life?

She gave him a wry smile. "Take care, Papa."

He released her, she moved away. He shook hands with Fernando. "Take care of them."

Fernando nodded. "I will."

Leaving the library without Fernando, Sophia walked to the kitchen. The smile faded on Concetta's face as Sophia said good bye.

"Are you all right, child?"

"I am. Thank you for taking care of him. I know it isn't easy." Sophia hugged Concetta.

Concetta held Sophia in place. "It's my job. Just that. No more, no less."

Hearing Fernando come up behind, Sophia broke free, left the house.

The pounding of footsteps on the path behind her made her slow her pace. She felt she couldn't get away fast enough.

Out of breath, Fernando caught up to her. "Hey. You okay?"

Turning to see him approaching her, sent her running into his arms. She held on to him like he was a life line. "I am now." Holding each other, they continued on down the path.

Reaching the rock barrier, as they climbed over, Sophia had an idea. "Let's go see the cave."

Fernando sat her down on the sand. "Okay. But we have a very nice bed to make love in now. I really don't want sand in my special places."

Laughing, she took his hand, jogged into their secret spot. She had come here the day before their wedding and cleaned it out. No more blanket, CD player or candles.

Entering the dark, damp area, she felt the chill she always got when they came here. Fernando wrapped his arms around her from the back, as she swayed against his body.

Sophia looked around the rock walls, dark and damp. "I will always love this place. Even empty and cold, it warms my heart."

Fernando spoke against her neck. "You are such a romantic."

She felt the comfort of his arms. "And you're not?"

His voice echoed in the cave. "I am, I admit it. You bring out the soft side of me."

She turned in his arms. "Oh, you macho man."

He drew her to him. "I am your man. For now and for..." She knew what he was going to say. "...ever."

"Forever." She laid her head on his chest, listened to the beating of his heart.

CHAPTER EIGHT

Sophia sat across from Jessica and Emily in the café.
Jessica shook her head. "I know the Italians don't celebrate Thanksgiving, but Emily and I do." She looked over at Emily. "Let's do it at my house."

Emily smiled. "You know I would love it. It's my first Thanksgiving away from home. Roberto is flying back, 'because everything is closed for this holiday'!"

Sophia shifted in her chair. Sometimes she had a hard time getting comfortable. "I think it sounds like a very nice holiday. A day to give thanks. We can all do that."

Jessica's face showed her delight. "Great then it's settled. My house, the last Thursday in November."

Uncle Sal walked out. "So what are you ladies plotting?"

Jessica leaned back. "Thanksgiving."

Uncle Sal nodded. "I've heard of that. It's a holiday in the States right?"

"Right." Jessica grabbed a pad. "Where can I get a turkey?"

"Alive?" Uncle Sal rested on one leg.

"Preferably not." She looked up at Sal. "Does Butterball mean anything to you?"

He frowned. "You put it on bread?"

Jessica shook her head. "Never mind. Emily and I will do the shopping."

Emily stopped Jessica's hand. "I have an idea. Let's have our mothers ship us everything for the normal feast."

"They would love it, maybe forgive us for not coming home." Jessica pointed her finger at Emily. "Good Idea, Cous."

Sophia didn't know much about this American Holiday, but she loved the idea of getting together.

***

Good smells greeted Sophia and Fernando as they entered Jessica's villa. Alejandro looked relaxed out of his white coat. Following the aroma, Sophia entered the kitchen. She stopped and looked at the array of food on the counter. Narrowing her eyes, she walked around stretching her neck to see what they were doing.

Together Jessica and Emily pulled a big roaster from the oven. Jessica lifted the lid and a puff of steam feathered up. "She's done." A large golden bird was lifted from the pan to a platter.

Jessica stood back took a breath. "We're ready."

Emily chuckled. "Why were you so nervous about this meal? You own a restaurant."

As she unsteadily carried the turkey to the table, Jessica sighed when she sat the heavy plate down. "I own an Italian café. Plus..." She turned to look at them. "I never cooked Thanksgiving dinner. We either went to Charles' folks or mine."

When Dreams Die

Sophia walked around the table looking at the food. "I hate to sound so country girl, but what is all of this?"

Jessica pointed at the dishes. "Sweet potatoes, oyster dressing, green bean casserole. Food of the Pilgrims."

Emily came to stand next to Sophia. "Yeah, right. Like the Pilgrims had little marshmallows."

Jessica smiled at the remark, yelling over her shoulder. "It's ready."

The men came to the dining area. Alejandro handed Sophia a glass of red liquid. "A little wine on a special occasion will do you good."

Grateful, she took a sip. The familiar taste rolled down her throat. She nodded her head. "Thank you."

Sophia looked around. Six places were set, but Roberto wasn't here yet. "Where's Roberto?"

Emily shrugged. "Seems there is a snow storm on the east coast. He's in the air now. He will be here soon." Sophia heard the disappointment in Emily's voice.

The yell of a small child redirected their attention. Jessica's baby girl sat in a high chair. Sophia admired the darling baby with the dark curly hair. She patted her stomach.

Soon. You and Tulia Bella will be playmates.

The front door burst open and in walked Roberto. Emily was immediately in his arms.

He lifted her and carried her to the kitchen. "I am here. And if I ever see snow again it will be too soon."

Hugs all around, then they sat at the table. Jessica instructed them to hold hands. In a quiet voice, she prayed. "Thank you, Lord. For family, health and peace. We are forever grateful."

Sophia looked up. They were all family in a way. And she was grateful. For each and every one of them.

A flutter moved in her stomach.

Okay, little one. I'm eating!

***

Sophia decided to work at home today. Early December, she was six months along. It was a chilly, rainy day. Dressed in sweats, a sweater and heavy socks, she built a fire, sat at her dining table and worked on her computer.

Matas brought her a cup of strong coffee. "Thanks. I will need this."

The TV was on for background noise and to keep tabs on the weather. The quiet rain could turn into a bad storm very quickly.

At lunch, she took a break. Stretching, she waddled over to the window that looked over the sea. Dark clouds gathered on the horizon. Hugging herself, she reflected on how different this Christmas would be from last year. They were going to spend it at Bella's. Paolo had agreed to come. They hadn't spent a Christmas together since they were small children.

Hugging herself, she noticed the rain hit her window with a sharp ping.

Ice.

The words on the TV alarmed her.

"We have a major pile-up on SP1...."

Sophia turned around to stare at the glaring screen picture of cars crashing into each other. A chill wrapped its icy fingers around her heart.

Fernando was traveling up that highway.

"Several fatalities at the scene. Help is having a hard time getting to the victims because of the amount of vehicles involved. The rain now has turned to ice."

Sophia sunk to her knees. "Matas!"

Matas came running. One look at Sophia, she was to her in a minute. "What is wrong?"

Sophia pointed to the TV. "Fernando. He is driving back..." the phone interrupted her words.

Matas grabbed it. Looking at who was calling before she answered, her voice trembled "Hello? Jessica?"

Sophia felt her stomach lurch. She didn't know what to look at. The TV was showing an aerial view of at least a half of a mile of battered cars. She shifted her look back to Matas, who was talking low to Jessica.

"Si. I will get her there." Matas disconnected the call. "Sophia..."

"Just tell me." Sophia was already up on her feet, her hands on her hips.

"Fernando was hurt. He is at the hospital. Alejandro is with him. I need to get you up there."

Before the last words were out, Sophia was headed for the door. Grabbing her boots, she sat on the bench to put them on. Grabbing her coat from the hook, she bolted out the door with Matas on her heels. The new Fiat they had just purchased stood ready to go. Sophia jingled the keys in her hand, then clinched them in her fist.

I need to drive.

Matas didn't challenge her. They entered the car at the same time. Sophia turned the key, paused took a deep breath.

I need to keep my head about me and just get to the hospital.

As soon as the car started to move, she felt the ice under the wheels. Pulling slowly out of the drive, she turned in the direction of the hospital. Thankfully the traffic was light, the hospital only a few minutes away. Matas sat still in the passenger's seat. Sophia glanced over at her and noticed she was gripping the bar on the door.

Stay calm, girl. I just need to get there.

The sign saying "Hospital" was a welcome sight. Pulling into the emergency parking lot, Sophia took the first parking spot. Jumping from the car, she didn't wait for Matas. When she felt her feet slip, she slowed down. Doing the shuffle walk, she grabbed hold of the cold metal bar of the door. Pushing it open, her feet met solid ground.

Now she could run. The blare of a siren chilled her. Coming up on the hustle of many gurneys with broken and bleeding bodies, she felt her knees start to go weak, her stomach churned.

Hang on. I need to find Fernando.

Reaching the desk, the girl behind it looked frazzled. While she tried to be kind and accommodating, her tone betrayed her impatience. "Can I help you?"

"Fernando Giordano?" Sophia gripped the edge of the counter.

While the girl was checking the computer, Matas caught up to Sophia. "Is he here?"

"I don't know yet." Sophia shook her head.

The girl looked up. "Yes, he is in examining room 10."

Sophia gave the girl a much deserved smile. "Thank you."

Looking at the numbers over the rooms, she wove her way through the mass of crying, damaged people. The nurses and doctors shouted orders, other hospital staff obeyed them.

7,8,9...

Her heart was in her throat.

10.

No thoughts preceded her entrance into the room, except...

Let him be alive.

The man in the bed turned to her. She gasped with disbelief. His face was bruised and swollen. "Fernando! Are you all right?"

He held out his hand. She eliminated the distance between them quickly. Taking his hand, she moved in to hug him, trying to be careful.

"I was so worried." She looked at his body. "You hurt?"

The voice of Alejandro sounded behind her. "He has a broken arm and a dislocated shoulder. Some cuts, bits of glass in his skin. He needs to go to surgery."

Sophia gripped his hand as she swayed.

I need to stay alert.

Alejandro steadied her, shouting over his shoulder. "Jessica!"

Sophia felt her friend take her by the shoulders. "Come on girl, we need to get out of the way."

Sophia nodded, looking into Fernando's eyes. She could see the pain he was in. Leaning down, she kissed him, then let Jessica move her away as they came in to get him.

***

Even the strong coffee could not keep Sophia awake. Jessica had taken her to a small private waiting room, then went to find Matas. As they sat waiting, Emily and Lucca came. Uncle Sal showed up explaining he had left Josh in charge of the café. Sleep came over her quickly. When she woke it took a minute to realize where she was.

The hospital.

Blinking her eyes, she looked around the room. Everyone was still there. Rising slowly. "How is he?"

Jessica looked over sharply, biting her bottom lip. "We haven't heard. So hopefully, no news is good news?" She raised an eyebrow.

Sophia pushed her hair out of her face. Looking around, she didn't see a clock. "What time is it?"

Emily looked at her watch. "It's four thirty."

Sophia frowned. "How long as he been in surgery?" She sat up straight now.

Jessica and Emily exchanged looks. "Three hours."

"Isn't that a long time for just some broken bones?"

Jessica pursed her lips. "I don't think so..." She looked down shook her head. "...I really don't know." She looked up at Sophia. "Do you need anything? Food? Coffee?"

Sophia stretched her neck. "The bathroom. Maybe some water." She pushed off from the sofa.

Jessica stood, pointed to a small room off to the side. "I'll get you some water. Hungry?"

Sophia shook her head, but her stomach rumbled.

Jessica must have heard it. She turned to Matas. "Did she eat lunch?"

Matas shook her head. "No we left before."

Jessica placed her hands tenderly on Sophia's shoulders. "Go to the bathroom. I'll get you something to eat."

Sophia didn't argue, just nodded. She went into the little room. Looking at herself in the mirror, she saw dark circles under her eyes. But more than that, she saw fear in her eyes. The baby kicked.

I know honey. I'm scared too. But we must believe he will be okay. He's our life.

Turning the handle, she walked back out into the room full of people. At a small table in the corner sat a bowl and a large glass of iced water. Jessica was fussing over the spot, but when she saw Sophia, she pulled out the chair. "Sit and eat."

Sophia had to smile at the commanding tone. Running the café had made Jessica somewhat bossy, but it was done with love. So Sophia forgave her.

Uncle Sal came over and looked down at the soup. "You call that a meal?"

Jessica put her hands on her hips. "It's the best they had."

"Ump! If we are here any longer, I will have food sent over from the café."

Sophia patted his chest as she slipped pass him to sit down. "Hopefully we won't be here much longer."

The soup, while inferior, did hit the spot. Her stomach gave another growl.

I'm eating.

As she ate, she listened to the small talk exchanged between Emily and Lucca. The low hum calmed her nerves. She could not imagine anything bad happening with so much love waiting out here. Finishing, she took her water bottle back to her seat on the sofa. Plopping down, the cushions felt good on her back.

Emily sat next to her, patted her knee. "He'll be fine. No need to worry. Alejandro is with him."

Sophia's mind went back to when the four of them were kids.

***

Roaming the small village, they were pretty much the kids to not mess with. As the four traveled the main street, people greeted them with smiles, knowing they would never cause any real trouble.

A group of teenagers stood across the street. Not from the area, they shouted out at them. "Hey kids. Where's some action around here?"

The boys circled Sophia. Roberto stood at the front. "What kind of action do you guys want?"

"A party would be nice."

Roberto shook his head. "Don't know of any..." His body stiffened. "...that would want scum bags like you."

The leader of the other group, walked straight to them. The others followed. "So, we have a tough guy?"

Roberto didn't back down. Alejandro came to his side. Fernando pushed Sophia behind him. Placing her hands on his waist, she leaned out to watch. The others were now across the street, standing in front of the boys. Sophia held her breath.

Not wanting to be the one to swing first, however when the leader tried to hit Roberto, he was blocked. Roberto hit him hard. Then the fight was on. Sophia backed up, but only slightly. One of the boys grabbed her. She doubled her fist and, with everything in her, connected with his face.

He yelled, released her. "You bitch...I'll..." as he started for her, Fernando grabbed the guy by the front of his shirt.

Backing him up, Fernando's face clouded with anger. "You will do nothing."

Since Fernando towered over him, the kid just looked at him. Fear creased his voice. "Okay dude. Nothing personal."

Fernando shoved the boy back into his friends. "Go away. There is nothing here for you."

The group scattered back across the street. Pulling at the car doors, they fell in. The driver gunned the motor and they tore out.

Fernando turned to Sophia. "You okay?"

She slipped into his arms. "Yes. Thank you."

They turned together. Alejandro was looking at Roberto's fist.

Sophia checked out the bleeding knuckles. "Is he okay?"

Alejandro patted the side of Roberto's face. "He's fine. Stupid but fine."

Roberto took his hand back. "What did you expect? They were wannabe tough guys."

Alejandro shook his head. "They were idiots." He walked over to Fernando. "You guys okay?"

Fernando pulled her close. "Yeah."

Alejandro patted her shoulder. "Nice right hook.

***

"Sophia." The soft voice of Alejandro stopped her daydreaming. She looked into his expressionless face.

Emily stood with her. Sophia swallowed. "Yes?"

"He's out of surgery." Alejandro looked around the room. "He's still critical."

Sophia took in a deep breath. "Why? He just had some broken bones."

Alejandro shook his head. "Sorry Sophia, I didn't tell you everything..."

Sophia felt the room start to spin. Emily grabbed her. She willed the room to stop.

Alejandro stepped towards her. "I had to think of you and the baby."

She braced her body into a fighting stance. "So tell me now."

"He had internal injuries, lots of bleeding. But I feel we fixed everything. He will just have a long recovery."

Sophia relaxed in Emily's arms. "Thank you." Without thinking she flew into his arms. Feeling the relief flow over her, she cried.

Alejandro held her. "It'll all be okay. He's a fighter."

Pulling back, she wiped her eyes. "Can I see him?"

"Sure." He took her arm, guided her down the long hallway to a secluded room. The lights were dim. In the bed, hooked up to several tubes, lay Fernando. His face was pale. She walked up to the bed alone.

Taking his hand, she rubbed it on her cheek, then kissed it. "You know I love you more than anything."

Nothing. He lay quiet. Still.

She looked around the room. Seeing a large chair in the corner, she placed his hand down on the bed. Walking around the bed to it she pulled it to the bedside.

Alejandro stood in the door. "Sophia. It is not good for you to stay here. I will be with him..."

She held up her hand "Shhh. Tell Uncle Sal I need food." She looked at Fernando, then back at Alejandro. "I'm staying."

CHAPTER NINE

Sophia juggled the brightly colored packages with both hands. "Do we have them all?"

Roberto and Emily had come over to help her load the car. Fernando was healing well, but he still moved with some pain. It had been less than a month since she almost lost him. Just the thought still chilled her to bone.

Roberto took the packages from her. "I think that's it."

Fernando stood in the doorway. Walking with a cane, he approached the car.

Emily finished putting things in the backseat. "I think you are good here."

Sophia walked over to her. "I wish you were riding with us." She looked back at Roberto. "Isn't it a bit cold to ride the bike?"

"It's okay, I have a car." Emily chuckled.

Sophia hugged her. "Good. I feel better."

Fernando walked with his cane up to the girls. "Thanks for the help Emily."

She hugged him back. "It is my pleasure. I am starting to feel like part of the family."

Sophia smiled. "You are part of the family."

When Dreams Die

Roberto snapped down the back hatch. Chapping his hands together he walked up to them. "What are we talking about?" He moved around the women to help Fernando in.

Sophia winked at Emily. "Family. And how nice it is."

He narrowed his eyes. "What are you telling her?"

Sophia gave him an innocent look. "Nothing, just talking." She walked around to the driver's side. "See you there. Drive safe."

Roberto put his arm around Emily. "You too." They both stepped back as the car pulled away.

Sophia looked over at Fernando. "Comfortable?"

He nodded his head. "Yes. I am glad you talked me into buying this car. More leg room than mine."

"Talked you in to it? Seems to me you were just as excited."

Fernando chuckled. "I was. Just, did we have to pick red?"

"What did you want? Another yellow? "She laughed. "They would look like mother and child." The picture in her mind was funny.

Fernando must have seen the same thing as he laughed with her. "I can see your point."

"Anyway..." She gripped the steering wheel. "Red makes me feel alive."

He reached over and took her hand. "That's what we are baby, alive."

***

Bella's villa was all decorated for the holiday. It was one of those dark winter days that could dampen the spirits, but the sight of all the sparkling lights make Sophia feel all tingly.

As she pulled up in front of the house, Deangelo and Marcello hurried down the steps. Sophia opened her door, stepped out, looked around the driveway. It was empty except for Alejandro and Jessica's car.

"Where is everybody?" She couldn't remember it ever being this vacant.

Marcello was lifting the luggage from the back seat. "It's just the immediate family for a few days."

Sophia grabbed a bag, which was immediately taken from her by Deangelo. "Go on in. We'll get everything to your room."

Uncomfortable with not being able to supervise, she gave directions. "The presents go under the tree..."

Marcello cut in. "No kidding."

She clamped her mouth. There would be time later to sort things out. Walking around the car, she took Fernando's arm. Speaking low so only he could hear. "They are going to mess everything up."

He leaned in and whispered. "It's all right. It's Christmas."

She gave him a smile. "You're right. Let's get you inside."

Alejandro met them half way up the steps. He stopped them. "You look good cousin. How are you feeling?"

Fernando tilted his head. "Better each day."

Alejandro turned to Sophia. "And you."

"Fat, bloated, tired."

Alejandro chuckled. "Normal for a pregnant woman."

When Dreams Die

Sophia twisted her lips. "We must be a sight. A bulging woman and a crippled man."

Jessica's voice reached them before she did. Coming around Alejandro. "You are both beautiful." Stepping in the midst of them, she took both of their arms.

Alejandro stepped aside. "Let me help the men." He looked at Jessica. "You okay here?"

Jessica nodded, started up the steps with her two charges. "We are fine."

Entering the house, the aroma of food was welcoming. The decorated house greeted them inspiring warm thoughts and good feelings. Jessica guided them into the kitchen. Bella and Gina were working at the stove. Fernando's mother, Orlinda, saw them first.

She dropped what she was doing and rushed to them, hugging them close. "My dears, how are you two?"

Fernando kissed his mother's cheek. "I am good, Mama. Every day is better."

Orlinda took hold of Sophia's shoulders. "And you dear?"

Sophia rubbed her now bugling belly. "Growing bigger every day."

"If you need to rest, go on up, dinner isn't for a couple hours."

Sophia looked around Orlinda's shoulders. "Is there anything to eat now?" Her manners and patience went out the window when it came to eating.

Bella spoke up from behind them. "Let the child through. If she is hungry, she must eat."

Sophia broke away from the other two and scooted up to the counter. With a bit of trouble she hiked up on the stool. "Whatcha' got?"

Gina and Bella immediately sat food in front of her. Picking up a fork, she let the first bite linger in her mouth. "Mmmm. Perfect." She gestured with two fingers together.

She felt Fernando come up behind her. She leaned back against him. "Hungry love?'

He kissed the top of her head. "Not now. I am going to join the men."

With her mouth full, she nodded. "Later."

***

Christmas Eve day Sophia walked along the beach to her father's house. The day was chilly, but sunny. She wanted to see her father alone. Maybe, just maybe they could have a conversation. Entering through the kitchen door, she found it dark and empty. Working her way into the rest of the house, she heard voices in the library.

Her father's voice was tense, almost angry. "...I bow to no one. I created this business, I will run it!"

Sophia pushed open the half closed door. "Papa?"

The two men in the room drew their guns.

Sophia raised her hands in front of her. "Whoa guys. I come in peace."

Vito motioned to them, they holstered the guns. He walked over to Sophia. "My dear, you startled us." He pointed his thumb at the men. "Sorry about that."

Sophia looked around her father. "Hey guys, how about taking a break?"

They both looked at Vito. He nodded, they left the room. Vito took Sophia's arm, led her to the sofa. Sitting down, he pulled her down with him. He looked down at her belly. "How are you?"

Sophia smiled. It pleased her he asked first about them. "We are good."

He raised his eyes. "And Fernando? After his accident?"

She figured he heard it from the people around about Bella's grandson. "He's good also."

The silence hung between them. Sophia looked around the room. "So where is Concetta?"

"I gave her two weeks off..." He must have seen her frown. "...with pay. She needs to be with her family during the holidays, not here caring for one old man."

Sophia for once saw the aging in her father. "Are you okay here?"

"Sure. I have my work and..." He frowned. "...it's enough.

Sophia took a road she never had before. "What is your work, Papa?"

Giving her a look of surprise, he scowled. "The winery. Making the best wine. What do you think?"

Shaking her head. "It just seems like you spend very little time working with the wine." She almost expected him to get mad.

Instead, he looked her in the eyes. "I have other interests."

She almost asked what but decided that would be pushing, so she stopped. Remembering the package in her hand, she held it up to him as a peace offering. "Here. Merry Christmas, Papa."

He took the present, tenderly opening the wrapping. Inside was a pocket watch. On the cover was an engraved picture of a grape field. As he pushed the button to release the cover, there was an engraving.

To Papa. All our love Sophia, Fernando and baby Raffaella.

He looked back up at her. Wetness formed in his eyes. "It's a girl."

Sophia nodded.

He looked back down at the watch. "You are naming her after your mother."

"Is that all right?" Sophia waited for the answer.

He snapped the cover closed. "Yes. That is nice."

Getting up, he walked to his desk, pulled open a drawer. Removing a small box, he came back to the sofa. Handing it to Sophia, he sat down, watching as she opened it. It was a beautiful white gold and blue sapphire rosary.

Sophia lifted it from the box. "Oh Papa, it is beautiful."

His face lit up with joy. "You like it?"

Slipping it over her head, she watched it fall down her breasts. "Yes, very much."

In a low, humble voice, he spoke. "I had it blessed by the Pope."

Sophia's eyes got big. "The Pope? In Rome?"

Vito smiled. "Yes. The big guy in Rome."

She was impressed. "How did you do that? What were you doing there?"

"We have been friends for years." He rubbed his forehead. "Confessing some of my sins."

Sophia didn't want to ask. She slapped her knees. "Hey, since Concetta is gone, how about some breakfast?"

He shrugged. "Sure. That sounds good. Can you cook?"

Sophia stood, took his hand and pulled him up. "I can."

Walking together to the kitchen, she directed him to sit at the small table in the corner. Knowing this kitchen as well as her own, she talked as she prepared an omelet.

"So, how's the crop this year?" She poured him a cup of coffee.

His face and body seemed relaxed. He looked out the window to the grape fields, now with leaves hanging dead on the vines. "Good it was good. How was Bella's?"

Sophia carried two plated to the table. Sitting down across from him, she shrugged. "Good I guess. I don't know."

Taking his first bite, he expressed his pleasure. "Mmm, this is good. So you do know how to cook." He cocked his head. "So you and Fernando are doing well."

"We are fine, Papa."

His face relaxed. "I'm glad."

Sophia narrowed her eyes and watched her father eat.

So he does care? Maybe.

***

Climbing back over the rock barrier, she saw Paolo leaning against the stones, his arms crossed. He turned at the sound of the pebbles falling. Holding out his arms, he lifted her on down.

"Paolo, why are you standing here?"

Taking her hand, they walked towards Bella's. "I was waiting for you."

"Why didn't you come over?"

He shook his head. "Not my thing."

Sophia walked in silence for a few steps, then decided it was time to ask questions. "He's getting old."

His tone was one of disinterest. "We all do."

"All he has is the business." Sophia didn't know why she found the need to defend him.

Paolo shrugged. "His choice."

Sophia jerked her brother to a standstill. "Why such contempt? He's your father too. And the business...I think he is in trouble."

Paolo looked her straight in the eyes. "His business? Is trouble."

"What is his business?"

Paolo looked away, off over the water, then back at her. "What did he tell you?"

"The winery. Some other interests." Her eyes begged him for the truth.

His hand cupped her face. "Leave it at that, Sis. It's better."

She started to speak, but his eyes told her not to. "Okay. For now."

They started walking again. Paolo looked down at her belly. "So how's the kid?"

Sophia grinned at him. "She is fine."

Paolo smiled. "A girl." He nodded his head.

Sophia rubbed her circles on her belly with her free hand. "We are going to name her Raffaella." She took a sideway's glance at him. Thought she saw tears in the corner of his eye.

He nodded again. "That's nice."

***

Christmas Eve was a huge affair at Bella's Villa. Many friends, all the family, extended, distant or otherwise came for the party of the year. Little children ran around, many babies cried or slept in one of their parent's arms.

Sophia had attended the party for years, so the amount of people did not surprise her. The feeling that it was her first as Fernando's wife did. Always on the out skirts. She remembered Fernando walking her home and her wanting to stay. So the fact that tonight she would be staying to be here first thing in the morning filled her with delight. Sitting at her normal spot at the table next to Fernando, she looked around at all the familiar faces. Next to her sat Emily.

Sophia patted Emily's hand under the table. "You okay with all of this?"

Emily looked at her, smiled. "How did you know I was overwhelmed?"

Sophia smiled. "I've been there."

Emily frowned. "But you have always been a part of this family. This can't be new to you?"

Sophia looked back at the people. "It feels like the first time and it feels like old times." She wrinkled her nose. "Does that make sense?"

Emily took hold of Sophia's hand, shook it. "It kind of does. This is the first year it is official."

Sophia nodded. "Something like that." Turning to Fernando. "Hey you."

He turned to her with a smile on his face. "Yeah." His slow steady way always brought feelings of love to her heart. "How was your visit with your father?"

Sophia thought back to the time in the kitchen. "You know, it was really good." She frowned. "Different."

"How so?"

"It was just the two of us. We sat in the kitchen and talked. Never did that before."

Fernando drew back, a skeptical look on his face. "Really? So all is good?"

Sophia thought of the uneasy feeling that passed over her. She shrugged it off then, but now it nagged at her. "I don't know. There is something about his business that doesn't feel right."

Fernando brushed off her concern. "What could be wrong with growing grapes?"

Paolo on the other side of Fernando, leaned out to see Sophia. "Sis don't fret over something that is not your concern."

While the words were spoken in a humorous tone, they stung.

Why would my father's business not be my concern? I will take this up with Paolo later.

CHAPTER TEN

New Year's Eve started around five in the evening at Bella's. Sophia took one last whirl to look at herself in the mirror. The affair was always formal. Her choice this year was a white and gold maternity dress. Going into the dress shop, she had felt foolish wanting such an elaborate dress. But between her and the sales clerk they had found the perfect dress at a reasonable price. Looking at it now, she felt it was worth it.

Fernando came up behind her, circled her waist, kissed her neck. Looking at the reflection in the mirror, she leaned back into his body. He was dressed in a black tux, looking ever so handsome.

"We look good, lovely lady." His voice warmed her soul.

Turning in his arms, she wrapped her arms around his neck, pressing against him. "We do. Have I told you today how much I love you?"

He kissed her long and deep. "First time today."

"Then I am sorry. You should be told every day." She snuggled into his arms.

"And if I remember right, I told you today. Didn't I?" He wrinkled his brow.

Going up on her tiptoes, she spoke against his lips. "Tell me again."

His warm breath brushed her lips. "I love you, Sophia."

The simple words said it all. She loved and was loved. That was all that was needed. Going downstairs, they were greeted by Lucca, Jessica and Alejandro.

"Happy New Year." They all shouted at the same time.

Paolo entered the room. Sophia took in a breath. Her brother looked so good in his tux. Sometimes she forgot how handsome he was. He kissed her cheek. Grabbing a flute of champagne that floated through the room on silver trays, he frowned at her.

She shook her head. "Dr. Alejandro said I could have half a glass at midnight."

A waiter appeared at her side, handing her a glass. "Sparkling cider."

She nodded. "Thank you."

Alejandro walked over to them. "Did I hear my name?"

Sophia raised her glass to him. "Just saying I am following doctor's orders."

Jessica came up behind him. "Might as well." She slipped into her husband's arms. "He knows best."

Sophia took a sip. "Where's Tulia?"

Jessica shook her head. "Asleep I hope."

Bella and her children entered the room. Suddenly, the noise level spiked. Sophia walked around Paolo and took a seat. "So brother, did you go see our father?"

Paolo sat down next to her. "No."

The simple answer stirred a response in her. "Paolo, we need to end this. Mother left. He stayed. We have to give him credit for that."

Paolo's face twisted in anger. She could tell he was holding back. He started to say something, then stopped. He got up and walked to the window. She could tell by the stiffness of his shoulder, he was holding back his rage.

She couldn't let it go. Standing, she spoke louder than she expected. "Paolo. If there is something I should know, tell me."

He kept his back to her. She walked over to him and turned him around to face her. "What? Am I wrong?"

Paolo looked pass her. The people in the room had become quiet. They were gathering around the brother and sister. Lucca came up between them.

He looked at Paolo. "Tell her. She deserves to know."

Sophia frowned at Lucca's words. "Does everyone know something but me?" She felt Fernando's hands on her shoulders. She braced herself for bad news.

Paolo glared at Lucca. "Why? It's not anything that can be changed."

Lucca got in Paolo's face. "Because it cost me my wife. If you don't tell her I will."

Paolo clinched his jaw.

Sophia took hold of Lucca's arm. "What do you mean?"

Lucca's expression softened as he looked at her. "Nerina and your mother were best friends. She was going to get your mother, when she had her accident." He spat out the last word.

Sophia looked at Paolo. "What does he mean?"

Paolo took a deep breath, took her hands. Looking down at them, he raised his eyes slowly. "Our mother didn't leave. She was banished from our lives."

This strung like a slap across her face. "Banished? What the hell does that mean?"

"Our father threw her out. She was not allowed to return or see us."

Sophia felt the bile rise in her throat. "How do you know this?"

"Because I went with her that night. I witnessed the whole argument."

Sophia felt the adrenalin shoot up her body. "Why didn't you stop him?"

"For god sakes. I was fifteen." Paolo ran his hand through his hair. "The only thing we could do was to leave."

"Why didn't you come and get me?" Sophia's fists were clenched. Anger flaring through every part of her body.

Paolo faced her, his voice edged with contempt. "He and his goons wouldn't let us." His body flexed. His face fell. "We wanted to. We tried later, many times, but he wouldn't let us." Tears formed in his eyes. "It broke her heart."

Sophia jerked away from Fernando's hold. "Well, we'll see about that." She headed for the door.

Bella stepped in front of her. "Sophia, it's done. It has been done for years. Let it go. Think of your baby."

When Dreams Die

Sophia's rage had now brought on tears of anger. "You all knew?" She swept the room with her eyes. Everyone stood still, quiet. "Well, he is going to answer for this. And I am going to find my mother."

Running, she pushed against the double doors. The cold of the night hit her bare shoulders. But she kept going. Down the stairs, to the beach.

She heard Paolo behind her yelling. "You can't. She's..." His words were swept away by the forceful sea wind. She kept running. Her chest hurt, fighting for air. Reaching the rocks, she tore her dress as she climbed over. Once on solid ground she ran to the house. The kitchen was dark, but she didn't even stop as she headed for the library. The light told her he was in there. Bursting through the doors, she stood before him with a powerful hate building.

"You banished her? What the fuck do you mean, you banished her?"

Vito faced her, waving his men away. "She disobeyed the code. She had to be barred from putting the family in danger."

"And what family is that, Father? Am I not part of the family?"

"Understand. I have rules I need to..."

"Shut up. I don't care about your rules, or codes or anything other than finding her. Where is she? And don't tell me you don't know. You know anything you want."

"She...she committed suicide when I forbid her from seeing you."

The anger rose like a bitterness to her mouth. If she had a gun she could have easily shot him with no qualms at this moment.

Her eyes shot fire at him. Her hands curled into fists at her side. "You bastard." Her voice was low, steady a sign of pure fury. She rubbed her round stomach. "This baby? You will never see her. We are dead to you, just like my mother. Die here alone, old man. I hope you rot in hell."

He started for her, put she put up her hands. "Don't."

He stopped. His face was distorted with pain, but she didn't care. Her pain was deeper, sharper and she had no room to consider his. Backing away, she glared at him, dared him and his goons to stop her. She felt the tears start in her eyes. She willed them back. Crying would come later. Right now she boiled with rage. Reaching the front door, she turned her back to him to open the large heavy door.

"Sophia. Please." His voice quivered. "Forgive me."

Sophia leaned her head on the wood. "Never Father. I will never forgive you."

Jerking open the door, she quickened her pace down the steps. Reaching the bottom, she realized she had not driven. The first car in the circle was her father's. Going to it, she found the keys in the ignition. Starting the car, she looked in the rear view mirror and saw her father on the top of the steps, watching her.

She put the car in gear, grabbing the seat belt to lock over her chest. Flooring the gas pedal, the wheels sprayed tiny rocks as she sped out of the driveway. Too mad to cry yet, she turned right towards Bella's. Fernando would be there. He would fix this.

Speeding down to the valley, Sophia heard a pop, pop, the window next to her shattered. A searing pain gripped her side, just under her arm. She couldn't hang on to the steering wheel. All of a sudden her car went out of control, hitting the guard rail, breaking the barriers. A ditch on the other side gave the fast traveling car just enough incline to fly into the air. Hitting the rough terrain on the other side it flipped over three times, before it came to rest upside down. Blackness surrounded Sophia's mind. Pain radiated from all parts of her body. She heard distant voices.

"There's a girl in there!" A woman's shouts cut through the pain and darkness.

Sophia forced her eyes open. She was upside down, held in her seat by the safety belt. A thud on her door, made her turn her face towards the shattered window. The welcome face of a middle aged man peaked back.

"She alive!" He shouted over his shoulder. His face was kind, his voice comforting. "You'll be alright, honey. Help is coming."

Sirens drew closer. Sophia could not begin to identify where she hurt, but one pain caught her sharp in her stomach, lasted a few seconds, then stopped.

I'm in labor! Oh my God, please protect my baby.

The grinding sound of crunching metal shook the whole car. She felt the freedom of the door being removed. A man in blue cut the belt, as another man held her, gentling removing her from the twisted metal prison. The two men lifted her up on to a gurney. Feeling the flat surface beneath her back, she grabbed for one of the man's hand.

"My baby!" Her words begged for help.

His eyes grew big as he followed her body to her bulging belly. "She's pregnant!" He shouted to the other men. A gripping pain shot through her. She put a death grip on the man's hand. He covered her hand with both of his. His eyes bore into hers. "She's in labor."

As the pain subsided, she released the pressure, closed her eyes and prayed.

Please God save my baby!

Tears and terror over took her.

Fernando! Help me! Fix this, oh please God fix this.

Lost in fear and her own pain, she faintly heard the voices of the medics, but then the words hit her hard.

"She's been shot."

As they worked over her, a policeman climbed in the ambulance. "That's Vito Rossi's car."

Sophia looked into the eyes of a person from her childhood.

"And this is his daughter." The young officer knelt down to look at her. "Sophia?"

Sophia gritted her teeth. "Find Fernando. He's at Bella's."

The man nodded, another sharp pain cut into her stomach, her back, on down her legs. She screamed as it took hold and threatened to never let go. But it did, and when she could breathe again, she felt the movement of the vehicle. Darkness over took her again as a mask was placed over her mouth. In the abyss she felt free of pain. Her body floated upward towards a bright light. The peace was welcoming. Clutching her stomach, she was startled to feel the flatness.

A deep voice spoke through the lights. "Go back. Your child needs you to survive. We will bring you back when the time is right."

The fact her child needed her was enough for Sophia to reenter the frightening world of pain. The ceiling above her sped by flashing lights in her eyes. The moving bed she was on turned a corner.

Vaguely the face of Alejandro appeared. "Sophia. Hold on. We'll get you through this."

The movement stopped, she was lifted onto another flat surface. She was cold, shivering. A familiar figure rushed to her side.

Fernando. Thank you God.

He took her hand. She could see the panic in his eyes. Clasping his hand for strength, she felt a giant pain rock her body.

A voice echoed up to her. "Push!"

Gripping Fernando's hand, she bared down with the little strength she had left. A wail from an unknown source crashed over her in a heat of love.

"You have a daughter."

She let go of his hand. In a state of painless bliss, Sophia watched as they placed the small baby into his arms. Suddenly she was aware she was floating and her body felt again whole. The bright light surrounded her, looking down she watched as Fernando held their daughter, unaware Sophia was leaving him.

A soft familiar voice sounded above her. "Come my daughter."

Tearing her gaze from her husband and child, she saw Raffaella. "Mama?

The smile that she had burned into her mind so she wouldn't forget, greeted her. "Yes Darling."

Sophia reached out and touched the welcoming hand of her mother. "Am I dead?"

"Yes."

"But Fernando? My daughter?"

"You will always be with them, just as I have been with you."

Sophia heard Fernando's voice announce. "Her name is Raffaella." The clock on the wall showed one minute pass midnight.

As she looked back she saw him look at her lifeless body. Hearing his screams, feeling his pain, she stopped her ascent.

"Will they be okay?"

"They will. You and I will always be there for them. To guide and protect."

Sophia nodded, then allowed her spirit to go into bright light.

EPILOG

Emily stood by the hospital window, looking outside. The evening dusk was dry and clear. She thought such a beautiful day should not be marked with such tragedy. Suddenly, she straightened up as fear gripped her stomach. One of Vito's distinctive black sedan pulled into the parking lot. She looked around, surveying the room. Fernando was over by the wall waiting for the doors to open and tell him the news, good or bad. Roberto and Paolo stood next to him. Jessica sat in a chair next to the window. Emily got her attention in a quiet way. Jessica stood, moved to Emily's side.

Emily pointed to the three men walking up to the main entrance. "Vito."

Jessica took hold of Emily's shoulders. "Oh my god. This is not good."

Both turned to look at the men. Emily got Roberto's attention first. She mouthed "Vito", just as the elevator doors dinged open. Roberto had his hand on Fernando's arm as they both turned towards the sound.

Fernando's face drained of its color. His first reaction was to lunge at Sophia's father. "You bastard."

Vito and his two body guards stopped, standing like an impassable wall. Roberto griped Fernando's arm, holding his cousin back.

Paolo moved to block his father.

Vito gruff demeanor crumbled before them. "You know I love her more than life itself."

Fernando tried to pull free, but Roberto held tight.

Paolo moved into Vito's space. He spat the words at the man he hated most in the world. "She was in your car. Someone wanted you dead. Only they shot the wrong person."

Vito moved forward, motioning his men back. He faced Paolo. "You're right. It was meant for me."

The doors behind them opened, Fernando turned to see Alejandro walk out. The expression on his face said it all.

"She's failing fast. We are going to try to save the baby. Do you want to be in there for the birth?"

Fernando took hold of his cousin's arms. "Yes."

Together, Alejandro and Fernando followed another doctor. A nurse handed Fernando a gown to cover his clothes, a masks for his face. Entering the operating room, Fernando saw Sophia laying unmoving on the table, several tubes running around her head. She looked beautiful, the angelic face full of peace.

The doctor directed Fernando to Sophia's bedside. He asked Alejandro to assist him. "She's weak, but I need her to push."

Fernando took Sophia's hand, leaned down next to her ear. "Honey listen to me. Your daughter needs you to bring her into the world. I am here to welcome her. Help me."

Fernando felt a squeeze, then Sophia's body pushed. Her eyes opened and she smiled at him. Then they closed and the monitor gave off the dreaded one continuous beep.

"I have her." The doctor's words were full of surprise.

A whale from the child let them all know she had arrived.

Sophia's hand fell away. Fernando turned to looked at the lovely girl he had always loved. The tears came quickly and heavy. But the nurse put the bundle into his arms and through the blur of tears, he saw their beautiful child.

2